"I a

"Yes,   d
with command,

"No!"

'We're flying to New York."

"*You're* flying to New York! I'm going home."

Home?" His tone changed, became hard.
Really? Is that why you came out the door
ith a suitcase?" There was a gate ahead; he
owed the car as they approached it. "I told
u not to take me for a fool, Rachel. When
came down those steps your only thought
s to run. I'd bet you didn't even have a
tination. Well, now you do."

et this through your head, Your Highness.
re's not a way in hell I'm flying to New
k or anyplace else with you. If you think
y   can—you can pick up where you left off in
n   apartment—"

looked at her, his eyes cold. Then he swung
t e wheel to the right and pulled onto the
s oulder of the road.

assure you, Ms. Donnelly, I'm not the least
interested in you sexually."

that's your idea of an apology—"

's a statement of fact. What happened earlier
s a mistake."

Sandra Marton wrote her first novel while she was still in primary school. Her doting parents told her she'd be a writer some day, and Sandra believed them. In secondary school and college she wrote dark poetry nobody but her boyfriend understood—though, looking back, she suspects he was just being kind. As a wife and mother she wrote murky short stories in what little spare time she could manage, but not even her boyfriend-turned-husband could pretend to understand those. Sandra tried her hand at other things, among them teaching and serving on the Board of Education in her home town, but the dream of becoming a writer was always in her heart.

At last Sandra realised she wanted to write books about what all women hope to find: love with that one special man, love that's rich with fire and passion, love that lasts for ever. She wrote a novel, her very first, and sold it to Mills & Boon® Modern™ Romance. Since then she's written more than sixty books, all of them featuring sexy, gorgeous, larger-than-life heroes. A four-time RITA® Award finalist, she's also received five *RT Book Reviews* magazine awards, and has been honoured with *RT*'s Career Achievement Award for Series Romance. Sandra lives with her very own sexy, gorgeous, larger-than-life hero in a sun-filled house on a quiet country lane in the north-eastern United States.

Recent titles by the same author:

NOT FOR SALE
THE ICE PRINCE *(The Orsini Brides)*
THE REAL RIO D'AQUILA *(The Orsini Brides)*

Did you know these are also available as eBooks?
Visit www.millsandboon.co.uk

SHEIKH WITHOUT A HEART

BY
SANDRA MARTON

First published in Great Britain 2012
by Mills & Boon, an imprint of Harlequin (UK) Limited.
Harlequin (UK) Limited, Eton House, 18-24 Paradise Road,
Richmond, Surrey TW9 1SR

© Sandra Marton 2012

ISBN: 978 0 263 89048 8

Harlequin (UK) policy is to use papers that are natural, renewable
and recyclable products and made from wood grown in sustainable
forests. The logging and manufacturing process conform to the
legal environmental regulations of the country of origin.

Printed and bound in Spain
by Blackprint CPI, Barcelona

SHEIKH WITHOUT
A HEART

CHAPTER ONE

IT WAS the kind of night that made a man long to ride his favorite stallion across a sea of desert sand.

Black silk sky. Stars as brilliant as bonfires. An ivory moon that cast a milky glow over the endless sea of sand.

But there was no horse beneath Sheikh Karim al Safir. Not on this night. His Royal Highness the Prince of Alcantar, heir to its Ancient and Honorable throne, was twenty-five thousand feet above the desert, soaring through the darkness in the cabin of his private jet. A rapidly-cooling cup of coffee stood on a small glass-topped table beside him; his leather attaché case lay open on the next seat.

Minutes ago he'd started to go through its contents until he'd suddenly thought, what the hell was the point?

He knew what was in the case.

He'd gone through the contents endlessly during the last two weeks and then again tonight, flying from the British West Indies toward his final destination, as if doing so would somehow make more sense of things when he knew damned well that was not going to happen.

Karim reached for the cup of coffee and brought it to his lips. The black liquid had gone from cool to chilly.

He drank it anyway.

He needed it. The bitterness, the punch of caffeine. He

needed something, God knew, to keep him going. He was exhausted. In body. In mind.

In spirit.

If only he could walk to the cockpit, tell his pilot to put the plane down. Here. Right now. On the desert below.

Crazy, of course.

It was just that he ached for the few moments of tranquility he might find if he could take only one long, deep breath of desert air.

Karim snorted. His head was full of crazy thoughts tonight.

For all he knew, there would never be a sense of peace to be drawn from this land.

This was not the desert of his childhood. Alcantar was thousands of miles away and its endless miles of gently undulating sand ended at the turquoise waters of the Persian Sea.

The desert over which his plane was flying ended at the eye-popping neon lights of Las Vegas.

Karim drank more cold coffee.

Las Vegas.

He had been there once. An acquaintance had tried to convince him to invest in a hotel being built there. He'd flown to McCarran field early in the morning—

And flown back to New York that same night.

He had not put his money into the hotel—or, rather, his fund's money. And he'd never returned to Vegas.

He'd found the city tawdry. Seedy. Even its much-hyped glamour had struck him as false, like a whore trying to pass herself off as a courtesan by applying garish layers of make-up.

So, no. Las Vegas was not a city for him—but it had been one for his brother.

Rami had spent almost three months there, longer than

he'd spent anywhere else the past few years. He'd have been drawn to it like a moth to flame.

Karim sat back in his leather seat.

Knowing all he now knew about his brother, that came as no surprise.

He'd finally had to face the truth about him. Tying up the loose ends of his dead brother's life had torn away the final illusions.

Tying up loose ends, Karim thought.

His mouth twisted.

That was his father's phrase. What he was really doing was cleaning up the messes Rami had left behind, but then, his father didn't know about those. The King believed his younger son had simply been unable or unwilling to settle down, that he'd traveled from place to place in an endless search to find himself.

The first time his father had said those words Karim had almost pointed out that finding oneself was a luxury denied princes. They had duties to assume, obligations to keep from childhood on.

Except Rami had been exempted from such things. He'd always had a wild streak, always found ways to evade responsibility.

"You're the heir, brother," he used to tell Karim, a grin on his handsome face. "I'm only the spare."

Perhaps adherence to a code of duty and honor would have kept Rami from such an early and ugly death, but it was too late for speculation. He was gone, his throat slit on a frigid Moscow street.

When the news had come, Karim had felt an almost unbearable grief. He'd hoped that "tying up the loose ends" of his brother's life would provide some kind of meaning to it and, thus, closure.

He drew a long breath, then let it out.

Now, the best he could do was hope that he had somehow removed the stain from his brother's name, that those Rami had cheated would no longer speak that name with disgust...

Cheated?

Karim almost laughed.

His brother had gambled. Whored. He'd ingested a pharmacopoeia's worth of illicit drugs. He'd borrowed money and never repaid it. He'd given chits to casinos around the world, walked out on huge hotel bills.

The bottom line was that he'd left behind staggering debts in half a dozen cities. Singapore. Moscow. Paris. Rio. Jamaica. Las Vegas.

All those debts had to be settled—if not for legal reasons then for moral ones.

Duty. Obligation. Responsibility.

All the things Rami had scoffed at were now Karim's burden.

So he had embarked on a pilgrimage, if you could use such a word to describe this unholy journey. He had handed over checks to bankers, to casino managers, to boutique owners. He'd paid out obscene amounts of cash to oily men in grimy rooms. He'd heard things about his brother, seen things that he suspected he would never forget, no matter how he tried.

Now, with most of the "loose ends" gone, his ugly journey through Rami's life was almost over.

Two days in Vegas. Three at the most. It was why he was flying in at night. Why waste part of tomorrow on travel when he could, instead, spend it doing the remaining clean-up chores?

After that he would return to Alcantar, assure his father that Rami's affairs were all in order without ever divulging the details. Then, at last, he could go back to his own life, to New York, to his responsibilities as head of the Alcantar Foundation.

He could put all this behind him, the reminders of a brother he'd once loved, a brother who'd lost his way—

"Your Highness?"

Karim bit back a groan. His flight crew was small and efficient. Two pilots, one flight attendant—but this attendant was new and still visibly thrilled to be on the royal staff.

She knew only what everyone else knew: that the duty of settling his brother's affairs had fallen to him. He assumed she misread his tight-lipped silence for grief when the truth was that his pain warred with rage.

It was difficult to know which emotion had the upper hand.

"Sir?"

As if all that weren't enough, she couldn't seem to absorb the fact that he hated being hovered over.

"Yes, Miss Sterling?"

"It's Moira, sir, and we'll be landing within the hour."

"Thank you," he said politely.

"Is there anything I can do for you before then?"

Could she turn back the calendar and return his brother to life so he could shake some sense into him?

Better still, could she bring back the carefree, laughing Rami from their childhood?

"Thank you, I'm fine."

"Yes, Your Highness—but if you should change your mind—"

"I'll ring."

The girl did a little knee-bob that was not quite the curtsy he was sure his chief of staff had warned her against.

"Most certainly, Your Highness."

Another dip of the knee and then, mercifully, she walked back up the aisle and disappeared into the galley.

He'd have to remember to have his chief of staff remind

her that the world was long past the time when people bowed
to royalty.

Hell.

Karim laid his head back against the head-rest.

The girl was only doing what she saw as her duty. He,
better than anyone, understood that.

He had been raised to honor his obligations. His father
and mother had instilled that in him from childhood on.

His father had been and still was a stern man, a king first
and a father second.

His mother had been a sometime movie-star-*cum*-Bos-
ton-debutante with great beauty, impeccable manners and,
ultimately, a burning need to spend her life as far from her
husband and sons as possible.

She'd hated Alcantar. The hot days, the cool nights, the
wind that could whip the sea of sand into a blinding froth...

She'd despised it all.

In some of his earliest memories of her he stood clutching
a nanny's hand, holding back tears because a prince was not
permitted to cry, watching as his beautiful mother drove off
in a limousine.

Rami had looked just like her. Tall. Fair-haired. Intense
blue eyes.

Karim, on the other hand, was an amalgam of both his
parents.

In him, his mother's blue eyes and his father's brown
ones had somehow morphed into ice-gray. He had her high
cheekbones and firmly-sculpted mouth, but his build—broad
shoulders, long legs, hard, leanly muscled body—he owed
to his father.

Rami had favored her in other ways. He hadn't hated
Alcantar but he'd always preferred places of sybaritic
comfort.

Karim, on the other hand, could not remember a time he had not loved his desert homeland.

He'd grown up in his father's palace, built on a huge oasis at the foot of the Great Wilderness Mountains. His companions were Rami and the sons of his father's ministers and advisors.

By the age of seven he'd been able to ride a horse bareback, start a fire with kindling and flint, sleep as contentedly under the cold fire of the stars as if he were in the elaborate palace nursery.

Even then, twenty-six years ago, only a handful of Alcantaran tribesmen had still lived that kind of life, but the King had deemed it vital to understand and respect it.

"One day," he would say to Karim, "you will rule our people and they must know that you understand the old ways." Always there would be a pause, and then he would look at Rami and say, not unkindly, "You must respect the people and the old ways as well, my son, even though you will not sit on the throne."

Had that been the turning point for his brother? Karim wondered. Or had it come when their mother died and their father, mourning her even though she had spent most of her time far from him and her children, had thrown himself ever deeper into the business of governance and sent his sons away?

He sent them to the United States, to be educated, he said, as their mother would have wished.

With terrifying suddenness the brothers had found themselves in what seemed an alien culture. They'd both been brutally homesick, though for different reasons.

Rami had longed for the luxuries of the palace.

Karim had longed for the endless sky of the desert.

Rami had coped by cutting classes and taking up with a bunch of kids who went from one scrape to another. He'd barely made it through prep school and had been admitted to a small college in California where he'd majored in women and cards, and in promises that he never kept.

Karin had coped by burying himself in his studies. He'd finished preparatory school with honors and had been admitted to Yale, where he'd majored in finance and law. At twenty-six he'd created a private investment fund for the benefit of his people and managed it himself instead of turning it over to a slick-talking Wall Street wizard.

Rami had taken a job in Hollywood. Assistant to a B-list producer, assistant to this and assistant that—all of it dependent upon his looks, his glib line of patter and his title.

At thirty, when he'd come into a trust left him by their mother, he'd given up any pretense at work and instead had done what she had done.

He'd traveled the world.

Karim had tried to talk to him. Not once. Not twice. Many, many times. He'd spoken of responsibility. Of duty. Of honor.

Rami's reply had always been the same, and always delivered with a grin.

"Not me," he'd say. "I'm just the spare, not the heir."

After a while they hadn't seen much of each other. And now—

Now Rami was dead.

Dead, Karim thought.

His belly knotted.

His brother's body had been flown home from Moscow and laid to rest with all the panoply befitting a prince.

Their father had stood stiffly at his grave.

"How did he die?" he'd asked Karim.

And Karim, seeing how fragile the older man had become, had lied.

"An automobile accident," he'd told him.

It was almost true.

All he'd left out was that Rami had evidently met with his cocaine dealer, something had gone wrong, the man had slit his throat and a dying Rami had wandered into the path of an oncoming car.

And why go over it again? The death was old news. Soon "tying up loose ends" would be old news, too.

One last stop. A handful of things to sort out—

A dull rumble vibrated through the plane. The landing gear was being deployed. As if on signal, the flight attendant materialized at the front of the cabin.

Karim waved her off. He wasn't in the mood for her misplaced look of compassion. All he wanted was to put this mess behind him.

Moments later, they landed.

He rose to his feet and reached for his attaché case. Inside it was what he thought of as the final folder. It held letters from three hotels, expressing sympathy on Rami's death and reminders that he had run up considerable bills in their casinos and shops.

There was also a small envelope that contained a key and a slip of paper with an address scrawled on it in Rami's hand.

Had he considered putting down some kind of roots here?

Not that it mattered, Karim thought grimly. It was too late for roots or anything else that might have resembled a normal life.

He'd get an early start tomorrow, pay his brother's bills, then locate the place that went with the key, pay whatever was due—because surely the rent was in arrears despite the lack of a dunning letter.

And then all this would be behind him.

His chief of staff had arranged for a rental car and for a suite at one of the city's big hotels.

The car had a GPS; Karim selected the name of the hotel from a long list and drove toward the city.

It was close to one in the morning, but when he reached the Las Vegas Strip it blazed with light. Shops were open; people were everywhere. There was a frenzy to the place, a kind of circus atmosphere of gaiety Karim didn't quite buy into.

At the hotel, a valet took his car. Karim handed the kid a twenty-dollar bill, said he was fine with carrying his own things, and headed into the lobby.

The metallic sounds of slot machines assaulted his ears.

He made his way to the reception desk through a crowd of shrieking and laughing revelers. The clerk who greeted him was pleasant and efficient, and soon Karim was in an elevator, on his way to the tenth floor along with two women and a man. The man stood with an arm around each of the women; one had her hand on his chest, the other had her tongue in his ear.

The elevator doors whisked open. Karim stepped out.

The sooner he finished his business here, the better.

His suite, at least, was big and surprisingly attractive.

Within minutes he'd stripped off his clothes and stepped into the shower. He let the hot water beat down on his neck and shoulders, hoping that would drive away some of the weariness.

It didn't.

Okay. What he needed was sleep.

But sleep didn't come. No surprise. After two weeks of coming into cities he knew would hold yet additional ugly truths about his brother, sleep had become more and more elusive.

After a while, he gave up.

He had to do something. Take a walk. A drive. Check out the hotels where Rami had run up enormous bills—this place, he had made certain, was not one of them. Maybe he'd drive by the flat his brother had leased. He could even stop, go inside, take a quick look around.

Not that he expected to find anything worth keeping, but if there was something personal, a memento that said something good about Rami's wasted life, their father might want it.

Karim put on jeans, a black T-shirt, sneakers and a soft black leather bomber jacket. Deserts were cold at night, even ones that arrowed into the heart of a city whose glow could be seen for miles.

He opened his attaché case, grabbed the key and noted the scribbled address. A tag that read "4B" hung from the key itself. An apartment number, obviously.

The valet brought him his car. Karim handed him another twenty. Then he entered the address into the GPS and followed its directions.

Fifteen minutes later, he reached his destination.

It was a nondescript building in a part of the city that was as different from the Las Vegas he'd so far seen as night from day.

The area was bleak and shabby, as was the building itself...

Karim frowned. He'd connected to global positioning satellites often enough to know that when they worked they were great and when they didn't you could end up in the middle of nowhere.

Yes, but this was the correct address.

Had Rami run out of the ability to talk himself into the best hotels at some point during his time here?

There was only one way to find out.

Karim got out of the car, locked it, and headed toward the building.

The outside door was unlocked. The vestibule stank. The

stairs creaked; he stepped in something sticky and tried not
to think about what it might be.

One flight. Two. Three, and there it was, straight ahead.
Apartment 4B, even though the "4" hung drunkenly to the
side and the "B" was upside down.

Karim hesitated.

Did he really want to do this tonight? Was he up to what
was surely going to be a dirty hovel? He remembered the
time he'd flown out to the coast to visit Rami when he was
in school. Dirty dishes in the sink and all over the counters.
Spoiled food in the refrigerator. Clothes spilling out of the
hamper.

"Goddammit," he said, under his breath.

The truth was, he didn't give a crap about the apartment
being dirty. What mattered was that it would be filled with
Rami's things. The hotel rooms had not been; the hotels had
all removed his brother's clothes, his toiletries, and put them
in storage.

This would be different.

And he was a coward.

"A damned coward," he said, and he stepped purposefully
forward, stabbed the key into the lock, turned it—

The door swung open.

The first thing he noticed was the smell—not of dirt but
of something pleasant. Sugar? Cookies?

Milk?

The second thing was that he wasn't alone. There was
someone standing maybe ten feet away…

Not someone.

A woman. She stood with her back to him, tall and slen-
der and—

And naked.

His eyes swept over her. Her hair was a spill of pale gold
down her shoulders; her spine was long and graceful. She

had a narrow waist that emphasized the curve of her hips and incredibly long legs.

Legs as long as sin.

Hell. Wrong building. Wrong apartment. Wrong—

The woman spun around. She wasn't naked. She wore a thing that was barely a bra, covered in spangles. And a thong—a tiny triangle of glittery silver.

It was a cheap outfit that made the most of a beautiful body, though her face was even more beautiful...

And what did that matter at moment like this, when he had obviously wandered into the wrong place...and, dammit, her eyes were wide with terror?

Karim held up his hands.

"It's all right," he said quickly. "I made a mistake. I thought—"

"I know precisely what you thought, you—you pervert," the woman said, and before he could react she flew at him, a blur of motion with something in her hand.

It was a shoe. A shoe with a heel as long and sharp as a stiletto.

"Hey!" Karim danced back. "Listen to me. I'm trying to tell you some—"

She slammed the shoe against him, aiming for his face, but he moved fast; the blow caught him in the shoulder. He grabbed her wrist and dragged her hand to her side.

"Will you wait a minute? Just one damned minute—"

"Wait?" Rachel Donnelly said. "*Wait?*" The perv from the lounge wanted her to wait? Wait so he could rape her? "The hell I will," she snarled, and she wrenched her hand free of his, swung hard...

This time, the heel of the shoe flashed by his face.

That was the good news.

The bad was that he muttered something and now he wasn't defending himself; he was coming straight for her.

Panting, she reacted with all her strength, but he was too big, too strong, too determined. A second later he had both her wrists in his hands and she was pinned against the wall.

"Dammit, woman! Will you listen to me?"

"There's nothing to listen to. I know what you want. You were in the lounge tonight. I brought you drink after drink and I knew you were going to be trouble and I was right, here you are, and—and—"

Her breath caught.

Wrong.

This wasn't the guy who'd undressed her with his eyes.

That perv had been bald with squinty eyes behind Coke-bottle lenses.

This guy had a full head of dark hair and eyes the cool gray of winter ice.

Not that it mattered. He'd broken into her apartment. He was male. She was female. After three years in Vegas she knew what that—

"You're wrong."

She blinked. Either she'd spoken aloud or he was a mind-reader.

"I'm not here to hurt you."

"Then turn around and go away. Right now. I won't scream, I won't call the cops—"

"Will you listen? One of us is in the wrong apartment."

Despite everything, she choked out a laugh. The man scowled and tightened his hold on her wrists.

"What I'm trying to tell you is that I didn't expect anyone to be here. I thought this was my brother's apartment."

"Well, it isn't. This apartment is—is—" She stared at him. "What brother?"

"My brother. Rami."

The floor seemed to shift under Rachel's feet. She felt the

blood drain from her face. The man saw it; those cold gray eyes narrowed.

"You know of him?"

She knew. Of course she knew. And if this was Rami's brother—if this was Karim of Alcantar, the all-powerful, stone-hearted, ruthless prince...

"I'm going to let go of you," he said. "If you scream, you will regret it. Is that clear?"

Rachel swallowed hard. "Yes."

Slowly, carefully, his eyes locked to hers, he took his hands from her.

"Obviously," he said, "I was correct. This place *is* my brother's."

"I—I—"

"You—you, what?" he growled with imperial impatience. "What are you doing here? This apartment belongs to Rami."

It didn't. It never had. It was hers and always had been—though that hadn't stopped first Suki and then Suki's lover from moving in.

Now, thank goodness, they were both gone. She lived alone...

Oh, God!

Her heart, already racing, went into overdrive.

She didn't. She didn't live here alone—

"Who are you?" the man growled.

Who, indeed? Her head was spinning. She should have known this would happen, that, sooner or later someone would come.

His hand shot out and manacled her wrist.

"Answer the question! Who are you? What are you doing here?"

"I—I'm a friend," Rachel said. And then, because she

had no idea what this man knew or didn't know or, most of all, what he wanted, she said, "I'm Rami's friend. His very good friend."

CHAPTER TWO

KARIM'S mouth thinned.

Friend, hell.

She'd been Rami's woman.

His mistress. His girlfriend. Whatever she'd been, for once in his life Rami had apparently fallen for a woman who wasn't his usual type.

He'd been into flash. This woman's costume, whatever you called it, was flashy, and yet somehow or other she was not. There was something removed about her, something in those dark blue eyes that said, *Be careful how you deal with me*.

Perhaps that had appealed to Rami. The challenge of getting past the invisible barricade around her. Maybe that had made up for the fact that she didn't speak in breathy little sentences or flutter her lashes.

Rami had been a sucker for nonsense like that.

Karim couldn't imagine this woman doing either.

She was tough. Hell, she was fearless.

Any other woman would have screamed for help. Run shrieking into the night. Or, at the very least, begged an intruder for mercy.

She'd come at him with a weapon.

A rather unusual weapon, he thought with wry amusement. The stiletto-heeled shoe lay on the floor next to him; its

mate lay a few feet away. The thing could have done real
damage, considering that the heels had to be four or five
inches high.

"Stilettos are torture," a mistress had once admitted, but
she'd worn them anyway.

He knew the reason.

Women wore them because they knew damned well that
men loved the look those high, thin heels gave to a female
body: the slight forward tilt of the pelvis, the added length
of leg.

Not that Rami's woman needed anything to make her legs
look longer.

Even now, they seemed endless.

She had stockings on. Hose. Whatever you called sheer
black mesh that drew his eyes up and up to where the mesh
disappeared beneath that thong.

With stilettos or without them she was a fantastic sight.
Sleek. Sexy. All woman.

Why deny it?

She was beautiful, and he was sure it was natural. He'd
seen enough women who'd been surgically and chemically
enhanced until they were little more than mannequins.

Cheekbones implanted. Lips injected. Foreheads all but
immobilized and, worst of all, breasts that looked and felt
like balloons instead of soft, warm flesh.

This woman's breasts would feel just right in a man's
hands. The nipples would taste sweet on his tongue…

Karim felt his body stir.

Hell. He'd been too long without sex. Why else would he
react to her? She was beautiful, but she was—she had been
Rami's.

Besides, he liked his women to be…well, at least some-
what demure.

He was a sheikh from an ancient kingdom, a culture still

learning to accept some modern concepts about women, but he was also a man of the twenty-first century. He had been educated in the west.

He believed in male-female equality, yes, but some degree of diffidence was still a good thing in a woman. He doubted if this particular woman would even understand the concept.

Karim frowned.

What did any of that matter? Rami was dead. And it was time to get down to business. Tell her that her lover was gone—and that she had until the end of the month to vacate the flat.

She'd said it was hers, but surely only by default. She was here; Rami wasn't.

Still, he'd write her a generous check. It was the right thing to do. Then, tomorrow—today, he thought, glancing at his watch and seeing that it was past six in the morning—he'd make good on the rest of his brother's Las Vegas debts.

With luck, he'd be in Alcantar by the weekend. Then he'd return to Manhattan and get on with his life—

"Well?" the woman said sharply. "Say something. If you're really Rami's brother, what's your name? And what are you doing here?"

Karim blinked.

Indeed, that was the big question.

Did she know about her lover's death? He didn't think so. She spoke of him in the present tense.

Then what was the best way to tell her? Break it to her gently? Or just state the facts?

That might be the best way. Be direct. Get it over with.

For all her feminine looks—the mouth that reminded him of a rose petal, the up-thrust breasts, the gently curved hips— for all that, he couldn't imagine there was anything fragile about her.

She was still the picture of defiance, dark blue eyes flashing, chin raised, ready to fight.

He could change that in a heartbeat.

All he had to do was remind her that he held the upper hand.

And there was an easy way to do that.

He'd pull her into his arms, plunge one hand deep into that mass of silky gold hair, lift her face to his and take her mouth. She'd fight him, but only for a few seconds.

Then her skin would flush with desire. Her lips would part. She'd moan and surrender to him, and it wouldn't matter if her surrender was real or if she was playing a part because he'd carry her to the sofa, strip away the bra, the thong, the spiderweb stockings, and by then her moans would be not a lie because he would make her want him, open for him, move under him...

Dammit!

Karim turned away, pretended to study the wall, the floor, anything at all while he got his traitorous body under control.

No wonder Rami had kept this one, he thought as he swung toward her again.

"What is your name?" he said sharply.

"I asked first."

He almost laughed. She sounded like a kid squaring off for a schoolyard fight.

"Is it really that difficult to tell me who you are?"

He could almost hear her considering his request. Then she tossed her head.

"Rachel. Rachel Donnelly."

"Well, Rachel Donnelly, I am Karim." He folded his arms over his chest. "Perhaps Rami mentioned me."

Rachel struggled to hide her distress.

Her unwanted visitor had confirmed her worst fear.

Rami had, indeed, mentioned Karim. Not to her. He'd never said more than "hello" and "goodbye" to her—unless you counted the times he'd brushed past her and whispered how much he wanted to take her to bed.

Suki had told her all about Rami's brother.

Her sister had hated him, sight unseen.

Karim, Suki said, was the reason Rami had no money, the reason he would never be treated properly by their father, the King.

It was all because of him.

Karim.

Karim the Greedy. Karim the Arrogant. Karim the Prince, who had deliberately driven a wedge between Rami and his father. Karim the Prince, with no concern for anyone but himself, no greater wish than to stop anyone else from possibly inheriting even a piece of their father's fortune.

Karim, the Sheikh with no heart.

Rachel had not paid much attention to any of it until Rami and then Suki had taken off.

Rami had left first. No warning, no goodbye. One day he was here and the next he and his things were gone.

Suki, no surprise, had hung in as long as she had to. And when it had been okay for her to take off, she had.

All she'd left behind was a stack of unwashed clothes, a wisp of cheap perfume—

And the one thing that had never mattered to Rami or even Suki but only to Rachel.

After that, Rachel had begun to think about the man she'd never laid eyes on.

About what he knew. Or didn't know. About how he'd react if he ever learned of what Suki had left behind.

Still, she'd never expected him to turn up on her doorstep without warning.

From all Rami had told Suki, his brother traveled with a
staff of sycophants and bodyguards…but here he was.

Alone.

And treating her with barely concealed contempt when
he wasn't looking at her with lust in his wintry eyes.

Rachel knew that look.

A woman who wore an outfit like this, who served drinks
in a casino, was fair game.

She hated everything about her job. The customers. The
atmosphere. The clink of the chips.

This awful costume.

She'd balked at wearing it until her boss said, "You want
the job? Do what you're told and stop bitching."

The girls she worked with were even more direct.

"You wanna be Miss High and Mighty," one of them told
her, "go pick up dirty dishes at the all-the-pigs-can-eat buf-
fet."

Rachel had already done a turn like that. You couldn't pay
the rent and support Suki—because Suki certainly hadn't
supported herself—you couldn't pay the rent or anything
else with what she'd earned clearing tables.

So each day she gritted her teeth, hid herself inside this
sleazy costume and went to work where men pretty much figured she was available for lots more than taking their drink
orders.

She hated it, but then, that was how men were. No big
surprise there.

Then Rami had moved in. After a few months, when she
couldn't stand living with either him or Suki anymore, Rachel
had confronted her sister and demanded she and her boyfriend find a place of their own.

Suki had burst into tears and said she couldn't do that.
She was in trouble…

That "trouble" had changed everything.

Rachel could no more have tossed Suki out than she could have flown to the moon, and—and—

"Have you lost the ability to speak, Rachel Donnelly? I have no time to waste."

No time, Rachel thought, no time…

Oh, God!

She'd been so caught up in what was happening that she'd almost forgotten the hour.

The wall clock read six-fifteen.

She'd gotten off work two hours ago, same as always. Which meant that the reason she'd stayed in Vegas was going to turn up at the door in forty-five minutes.

She'd never been sure what she was going to do if and when this moment came.

She was sure now.

She was sure of something else, too.

Rami's brother knew nothing.

If he had, he'd have already demanded his rights to that which he surely would have seen as his.

"Such a fuss over wanting to know my name."

Rachel looked up. The Sheikh stood with his arms folded, a big, hard-faced, hard-bodied, cold-as-ice piece of work who just happened to look like a god.

Unfortunately for him she knew the truth: that he was a cold-hearted SOB who was an expert at manipulating people to see him as he wanted to be seen.

"Such a fuss," he said, his tone ripe with sarcasm, "and now you have nothing to say."

She squared her shoulders.

The thing to do was face him down and get him out of here.

"Actually, I just wanted to be sure. I'd already figured it out myself."

"Really?" he purred.

"Rami described you pretty accurately. Self-important. Arrogant. A despot. Yes, he got it right."

A hit. She saw a flush rise over those high cheekbones.

"You're a sheikh, aren't you? From Alashazam. Or Alcatraz. Something like that."

The imprints of color deepened. He took a step forward. Rachel fought the desire to retreat.

"Something like that," he said coldly.

"Well, Rami isn't here."

That brought a thin smile to his lips. Had she said something amusing?

"But I'll be sure and tell him you called. Now, Sheikh-Whatever-You're-Called, I'm busy. And—"

"I am called Prince Karim," Karim said stiffly. "Or Your Highness. Or I am addressed as Sheikh."

Damn. Was he actually saying this stuff? If there was anything he despised, it was the use of these outmoded titles, but this Rachel Donnelly brought out the worst in him.

"Yes, well, your Sheikhiness, I'll give Rami your message. Anything else?"

The way she'd combined his titles was an obviously deliberate insult. He wanted to grab her and shake her—

Or grab her and wipe that little smirk off her lips in a very different way—one that would change her demeanor altogether.

For all he knew, that was the reason she'd taunted him. A woman who looked like this would surely use sex to gain the upper hand.

He wasn't fool enough to let it happen.

"No?" she said brightly. "Is that it? Well, in that case, goodbye, good luck, and on your way out don't let the door slam you in the—"

"Rami is dead."

He had not intended to give her the news that abruptly but,

dammit, she'd driven him to it. Well, it was too late to call back his brusque words. He could only hope he'd assessed her correctly: that she was too tough to faint or—

"Dead?"

He'd guessed right. She wasn't the fainting type. Evidently she wasn't the weepy type, either. Her only reaction, as far as he could tell, was a slight widening of her eyes.

He was willing to be generous.

Perhaps she was in shock.

Karim nodded. "Yes. He died last month. An accident in—"

"Then why are you here?"

He had not really had the time to consider all her possible reactions to his news, but if he had, this—this removed curiosity would not have been on the list.

"That's it? I tell you your lover is dead and all you can say is, 'Why are you here?'"

"My lover?"

"The man who kept you," he said coldly. "Is that a better way to put it?"

"But Rami…"

Her voice trailed away. He could see her reassessing. Of course. She was trying to process the situation, determine what would do her the most good now that Rami was gone.

And he had been gone for a while.

She hadn't known he was dead but it had happened weeks ago, making that casual "I'll be sure and tell him you called" remark an obvious lie.

Why?

"But Rami…what?" Karim said coldly.

She shook her head. "Nothing. I mean, I just— I just—"

"He left you."

Rachel's mind was whirling and that blunt statement of fact only added to her confusion.

Rami was dead.

Did that make things worse? Did it make them better?

No. It changed nothing except to give her all the more reason to stay the course until she heard from Suki.

She gasped as Karim's hands closed on her arms.

"Why lie to me, Ms. Donnelly? We both know that my brother left you weeks ago."

Rachel looked up. She had never seen eyes more filled with contempt.

"Why ask me a question if you already know the answer?"

"What I know," Karim said, his mouth twisting, 'is that you don't give a damn that he's dead."

"You're hurting me!"

"How long did it take you to find his successor?"

She stared at him. "His—?"

"Another fool who'd keep you. Pay your bills. Buy what you're selling."

Her eyes flashed.

"Get out of my home!"

"Your home?" Karim raised her to her toes. "Rami paid the bills here. All you did was have the good fortune to warm his bed."

"If warming your brother's bed was an example of good fortune, heaven help us all!"

God, he wanted to shake her until she was dizzy!

Once, a very long time ago, he had loved his brother with all his heart.

They'd played together, told each other the secrets boys tell; they'd wept together at the news of their mother's death, bolstered each other's spirits the first weeks at boarding school in a strange new land.

That boy was only a memory... A memory that suddenly raised a storm of emotion Karim had kept hidden even from himself.

Now that emotion flooded through him, set loose by the coldness of a woman his brother had once cared for.

Karim had seen people show more sorrow at the sight of a deer dead on the road than Rachel Donnelly was showing now.

"Damn you," he growled. "Have you no feelings?"

Her eyes glittered with a burst of blue light.

"What a question, coming from a man like you!"

There was a red haze in front of his eyes. Karim cursed; his hands tightened on her.

"Let go of me!"

She slammed a fist against his shoulder. He caught both hands in one of his, immobilized them against his chest.

"Is that how you dealt with Rami?" he growled. "Did you drive him crazy, too?"

Mercilessly, he dragged her closer. Clasped her face in one big hand. Lowered his head toward hers...

And stopped.

What was he doing?

This was not him.

He was not the kind of man who'd force himself on a woman. Sex had nothing to do with anger.

No matter that she'd brought him to this, or that she was a grasping, heartless schemer. It didn't give him the right to treat her this way.

He let go of her. Took a step back. Cleared his throat.

"Miss Donnelly," he said carefully, "Rachel—"

"Get out!" Her voice shook; her eyes were enormous. "Did you hear me? Get out, get out, get—"

"Rachel?"

Karim swung toward the door. A woman, middle-aged, plump, pleasant-faced, looked from Rachel to him, then at Rachel again.

"Honey, is everything all right?"

Rachel didn't answer. Karim turned toward her. She'd gone pale; he could see the swift rise and fall of her breasts.

"Mrs. Grey." Her voice was a hoarse whisper. She looked at Karim, then at the woman in the doorway. "Mrs. Grey. If you could just—if you could just come back a little later—"

"I thought it was him at first," Mrs. Grey said, frowning. "Wrong hair color but same height, same way of standin'. You know who I mean? That foreigner. Randy. Raymond. Rasi. Whatever his name is."

"No." Rachel shook her head. "It isn't. Look, I hate to ask, but if you would—"

"Just as well, if you ask me. Good-lookin' man, but any fool could see right through him."

"Mrs. Grey." Rachel's voice was unnaturally high. "This—this gentleman and I have some business to conclude and then I'll—"

"Sorry, honey, but I'm runnin' late. Brought my daughter along today. She's gonna work the mornin' shift and I have to drop her off after I leave here. Save her takin' the bus, you know, and…" Her eyes over to Karim again. "This a new friend?"

"No," Karim said coldly, "I am not Miss Donnelly's friend."

"Too bad. You look a nice sort. Not like that Rasi." The woman shook her head. "Still, you'd think he'd come back, do the right thing by—"

"Momma? Honestly, you move too fast for me. You was up these stairs before I was half-started," a woman's voice said with a little laugh.

A younger version of Mrs. Grey appeared beside her.

She had something in her arms.

A blanket? A bundle?

Karim's breath caught.

It was a child. An infant—and it reminded him of some-one. Someone from long, long ago.

"You'd think a man would want to do right for his very own son and his mama, wouldn't you?" Mrs. Grey said to Karim.

Rachel Donnelly, who had shown no emotion at all at the news of Rami's death, made a little sound. Karim tore his eyes from the baby and looked at her.

She was trembling.

Carefully, he reached for the child. Thanked the two women. Said something polite. Closed the door.

Stared down at the baby in his arms.

And saw perfectly miniaturized replicas of his brother's eyes. His brother's nose.

And Rachel Donnelly's mouth.

CHAPTER THREE

THE world stood still.

Such a trite phrase, Karim knew, but it took a conscious effort to draw air into his lungs.

What he was thinking was impossible.

This child had nothing to do with his brother.

Eye color. The shape of a nose. So what? There were only so many shades of blue in the world and only so many kinds of noses.

He took a deep breath.

Okay.

He'd been at this too long. That was the problem. He had certain routines. Rami had teased him unmercifully about how boring his life must be, but a routine was what kept a man grounded.

Up at six, half an hour in his private gym, shower, dress, coffee and toast at seven, at his desk by eight.

He'd been away from that schedule for too long, flying almost non-stop from city to city, seeing all the unpleasant details of his brother's life unfold.

It was having an effect.

If Rami had fathered a child, he'd have known.

They were brothers. Out of touch, but surely a man would not keep something like that to himself...

"Blaa," the baby said, "blaa-blaa-blaa."

Karim stared down at the child.

Blah, indeed.

Of course Rami would have kept it to himself—the same as he'd never mentioned his gambling debts.

You didn't talk about your mistakes—and the birth of a child out of wedlock was a mistake.

Rami had scoffed at convention, but under it all he'd known he was the son of a king and, after Karim, next in line to the throne.

There were certain rules of behavior that applied, even to him.

News of an illegitimate child would have resulted in a scandal back home. Their father might have completely cut off his younger son, even banished him from the kingdom.

So, yes. The child was Rami's, and it was illegitimate. There had not been a marriage certificate among his brother's papers. There'd been lots of other stuff. Expired drivers' licenses. Outdated checkbooks. Scribbled notes and, of course, endless bills and IOUs.

Nothing that even hinted at a wife.

Rachel Donnelly stood before him, as frozen as a marble statue, her eyes locked on the child in his arms.

No. Rami had not married her. Drunk or not, he surely would have known better than to tie himself permanently to a woman like this.

She was a woman a man bedded, not wedded, Karim thought, without even a hint of humor.

Beautiful.

Fiery.

Tough as nails.

His brother might have found all that spirit and defiance sexy.

He did not and would not. But this wasn't about him.

"Give me the baby."

Her voice was low, a little thready, but the color had come back into her face. She was regaining her composure.

Why had she reacted with such distress?

If this was Rami's child, this could be a golden opportunity. Her lover's child and her lover's brother, coming face to face...

"Give me the baby!"

He wondered why she hadn't tried to contact him before this. Well, that was obvious. She'd thought Rami would come back to her.

Was this the reason he'd left her? Because she'd become pregnant?

It was an ugly thought, that his brother would have abandoned his own child, but nothing about Rami surprised him anymore.

Assuming, of course, the child was his.

How had his brother let this happen? Drunk or sober, how could he have forgotten to use a condom?

Had the woman seduced him into forgetting? That was always a possibility.

Karim wasn't naïve. A man who was born to a title and a fortune learned early how things went.

Women set snares; his own mother had been pregnant with him before his father had married her.

He wasn't supposed to know that, but any fool could count. And once he'd figured it out he'd had a better idea of why his parents' marriage had failed.

You chose a wife—especially if you had the responsibilities of a prince—because she met certain criteria. Common interests and backgrounds. Common goals and expectations.

You *chose* her; you didn't put yourself in a position where fate or expediency or, even worse, a foolish night of passion became the deciding factor—

A small fist hit his shoulder. Karim blinked in surprise.

The woman had moved right up to him. Her eyes flashed with anger.

"Are you deaf? Give—me—the—baby!"

The child made an unhappy sound. Its mouth, that mouth that was the image of hers, began to tremble.

Karim narrowed his eyes.

"Whose child is this?"

"What is this? An interrogation? Give Ethan to me and then get the hell out!"

"Ethan?"

Dammit, Rachel thought, she hadn't intended to give him anything—not even the baby's name.

"Yes. And he's wary of strangers."

Karim's mouth twisted. "Was he wary of my brother?"

"I'd tell you that you've overstayed your welcome, Your Sheikhiness, but you were not welcome here in the first place."

"Do not," Karim said grimly, "call me that."

He regretted the words even as he said them. It was a mistake to let her know she was annoying him because that was damned well what she wanted to do.

"I'll ask you again," he said, struggling to control his temper. "Who does this child belong to?"

"He belongs to himself. Unlike you and your countrymen, Americans don't believe people can be owned like property."

"A charming speech. I'm sure it will win applause on your Fourth of July holiday. But it hasn't got a damned thing to do with my question. Once again, then. Whose child is this?"

Rachel chewed on her lip.

Whose, indeed?

Suki and Rami had created Ethan.

But from the very beginning he'd been hers.

For Suki, the bump in her belly had been a nine-month

annoyance, especially once she'd realized she couldn't use her pregnancy to convince Rami to marry her.

He'd packed his things and taken off well before Ethan's birth.

It had been Rachel who'd held Suki's hand during labor, Rachel who'd cut the baby's umbilical cord.

When Suki and her son had come home from the hospital, the baby had cried endlessly. He'd been hungry; Suki had refused to nurse him.

"What," she'd said in horror, "and ruin my boobs?"

The formula hadn't agreed with him. He'd kept spitting up; his tiny diaper had always been full and foul-smelling. Suki had shuddered, and left his care to Rachel.

Rachel had been fine with that.

She'd changed his formula. Changed his diapers. The baby thrived.

And Rachel adored him.

She'd loved him even before he was born. It was she who'd come up with a name, who'd bought a crib and baby clothes. He was hers, not Suki's. And when Suki had finally left, Rachel was almost ashamed to admit she'd been happy to see her go.

Now everything was falling apart.

She had never worried that Rami might return and claim his son—even if he had, she'd sensed that he was a coward underneath the charm and good looks.

She could have faced him down.

But if this arrogant bully wanted Ethan...

"Ms. Donnelly. I asked a simple question."

The baby began to whimper.

"That's it," Rachel said. "Raise your voice. Terrify the baby. Is that your specialty? Walking into places you aren't welcome? Scaring small children?"

"I asked you a simple question, and you will answer it! Whose child is he?"

"You," Rachel said, stalling for time, "you are an awful man!"

His teeth showed in a wolfish grin.

"I'm heartbroken to hear it."

"What will it take to get you out of here?"

"The truth," he snapped. "Whose baby is this?"

Rachel looked straight into his cold eyes.

"Mine," she said, without hesitation, forcing the lie through a suddenly constricted throat, because Ethan *was* hers.

It was just that she hadn't given birth to him.

"Don't play games with me, madam. You know what I'm asking. Who is the father?"

There.

They'd reached the impasse she'd been dreading. Now what? She should have known he wouldn't be satisfied with her answer.

The Sheikh, the Prince, whatever you were supposed to call him, was not a fool.

Ethan looked like his parents. He had Rami's coloring and eyes, Suki's chin and mouth. Well, hers, too, because she and Suki resembled each other, but the Sheikh wouldn't know that.

He didn't even know Suki existed.

And she had to keep it that way.

"Answer me!"

"Lower your voice. You keep yelling—"

"You think I'm yelling?" the Sheikh yelled.

Predictably, Ethan began to cry.

The mighty Prince looked stunned. Evidently not even infants were permitted to interrupt a royal tirade.

"Now see what you've done," Rachel snapped, and scooped Ethan into her arms.

His cries became wails; his little body shook with outrage. The look on the Sheikh's face was priceless.

Under other circumstances she'd have laughed, but there was nothing to laugh at in this situation.

Instead, she walked slowly around the small living room, cooing to the baby, stroking his back, pressing kisses to his forehead.

His cries lessened, became soft sobs.

"Good baby," she whispered.

She felt Karim's eyes following her.

No way was he going to stop peppering her with questions. With *one* question.

Was Rami her baby's father?

And, yes, Ethan was hers. He always would be. She'd made the baby that promise the day Suki left.

Now that could change in a heartbeat.

Once she acknowledged what the Sheikh surely already suspected, her life, and Ethan's, would be in his hands.

He would surely decide to claim his brother's son. He was cold, yes. Heartless, absolutely. Rami had said so, and the last hour had proved it, and she could not imagine he'd feel anything for anyone, not even a baby.

Nevertheless, he'd never leave Ethan with her.

There was that whole royal bloodlines thing. Rachel had heard Rami whine about it to Suki. The fact that you were a royal was what set the path of your existence.

The Sheikh would demand custody and he'd get it.

He had money. Power. Access to lawyers and politicians and judges—people she couldn't even envision.

She had nothing.

This dark little apartment. Maybe four hundred dollars in the bank. A job she despised and, yes, she could just see how

"Occupation: half-dressed cocktail waitress" would stack up against "Occupation: powerful prince who spends the days counting his money."

The answer was inevitable.

He'd take Ethan from her.

Raise him as Rami had told Suki he'd been raised.

No love. No affection. Nothing but discipline and criticism and the harsh words and impossible demands of an imperious father and now, for Ethan, the demands of a heartless uncle.

A lump rose in Rachel's throat.

She couldn't let that happen. She *wouldn't* let it happen.

She'd do whatever was necessary to keep her baby—and there was only one way to accomplish that.

Show the Sheikh that he couldn't intimidate her, get him out the door—then pack a suitcase and run.

The baby's cries had faded to wet snuffles. Rachel took a breath and turned toward the Sheikh.

"He needs a new diaper."

"And I need answers."

"Fine. You'll get them when I have time. I'll meet you later. Say, four o'clock in front of the Dancing Waters at the… What's so amusing?"

"Did you really think I'd fall for such a stupidly transparent lie?" His smile vanished. "Change the child's diaper. I'll wait."

"Don't try to give me orders in my own home."

"It was my brother's home, not yours. You lived here with him. You were his mistress."

"Wrong on both counts. This apartment is mine."

"And my brother just happened to have the key."

His tone was snide and self-confident, and if it weren't for Ethan, she'd have slapped it off his all-too-handsome face.

"My mistake for giving him one. He moved in with me, not me with him. And, for the record, I've never been anybody's mistress. I've always supported myself and I damned well always will."

There it was again. Fire. Spirit. Absolute defiance. Her eyes were snapping with anger even as she kept her voice low for the baby's sake, kept stroking her hand gently down his back.

Karim watched that slow-moving hand.

The feel of it would soothe anyone. A child. A beast.

A man.

Without thinking, he reached out and touched the baby. His fingers brushed accidentally against the curve of the Donnelly woman's breast.

She caught her breath. Their eyes met. Color rushed into her face.

"The boy is asleep," Karim said softly.

"Yes. He is." She swallowed hard. He could see her throat arch. "I—I'm going to take him into the bedroom, change his diaper and put him down for a nap."

"Fine," he said briskly.

He watched her walk away with the dignity of a queen, back straight, only the slightest sway of her hips.

He wanted to laugh.

What an act! The personification of dignity in a cheap costume.

It was an act, wasn't it? The way she held herself. The love she seemed to show the baby. Her adamant refusal to name Rami as the child's father, as if she suspected what Karim's next move would be.

She wasn't stupid; far from it. Surely, she knew he would demand custody of the boy.

And he would get it. A DNA test, quickly performed, would settle things.

She was—whatever she was. A dancer. A stripper. She was broke or close to it, judging by where she lived.

And he was a prince.

There was no doubt which of them would win in a court of law—if this ever got that far.

But there was no need for that to happen.

Rachel Donnelly would not give up the child without a fuss. If he were generous, he'd say it was because she cared for the boy but he was not feeling generous. He was feeling deceived. By Rami. By fate. And now, for all he knew, by a woman who was an excellent actress, making a show of being a caring mother.

Whatever her motive, she could not be permitted to keep the boy.

That was out of the question.

He would not leave the child to be raised in squalid surroundings by a woman who, at best, might euphemistically be called a dancer.

With him, the boy—Ethan—would have everything Rami could have given him. A comfortable home. The best possible education. The knowledge of his ancient and honorable past.

He would not have a mother but Rami had not had one, either. For that matter, neither had he, and he was none the worse for it today.

Karim looked at the closed bedroom door and frowned. What was taking her so long? Changing a diaper could not be a complicated procedure.

Did she expect him to stand here, cooling his heels?

He had things to do. Settling Rami's debts, of course. And now he'd have to make arrangements for taking the child to Alcantar. What would he need? Clothes? Formula? The boy's birth certificate?

Not really.

He had diplomatic status. Only the State department had the authority to question him, and they would not do so.

What else would he require?

Of course.

A nanny.

That was the primary requirement. A woman who'd be capable of knowing a baby's needs. She could care for the boy from now until Karim had him back home, where he could make more permanent arrangements.

Relatively simple, all of it.

Assuming Rachel Donnelly didn't cause trouble—but why would she? He would write her a handsome check and if she balked he'd make her see how much better off her son would be in his new life as a prince in his father's kingdom.

He might even agree to permitting her to visit a couple of times a year—

And, dammit, he was wasting time!

Karim strode to the closed door and rapped his knuckles against it.

"Miss Donnelly?"

Nothing.

"Miss Donnelly, I cannot spend the entire morning waiting for you. I have other business to conduct."

Still nothing.

Hell.

Was it possible there was another exit from the apartment? A window that opened on an outside stairway?

Karim flung the door open.

The furnishings were spare.

A chest of drawers. A chair. A crib, Ethan sound asleep in it, his backside in the air.

And a bed.

Narrow. Covered in white. The only color came from the bra, the thong, the dark mesh stockings that lay in a tiny heap in its center.

His belly knotted.

His gaze flew to a half-open door, wisps of steam curling from it.

The sound of running water drummed in his ears, or was it the beat of his pulse?

Get out of this room, a voice within him whispered. *She's in the shower, naked. You don't belong here.*

Instead, he took a step forward. Then another.

Ah, God.

He could see into the bathroom. Into the small stall shower. Condensation clouded the glass but he could see her. See her as Matisse or Degas might have painted her—just the hint of that lovely face, that exquisite body.

The water stopped.

Get out, he thought again, but his feet seemed rooted to the floor.

She slid the shower door open.

And he saw her without the glass.

Her hair, wet and streaming over her shoulders, almost hiding the rounded perfection of her breasts.

Her waist, surely narrow enough for his hands to span.

Her hips, ripely curved.

Her legs, long enough so he could almost feel them wrapped around him.

And the golden curls at the juncture of her thighs, guarding the female heart of her.

She didn't see him. Wet strands of her hair hung over her eyes.

He watched as she reached toward the towel rack, her hand fumbling for a white bath sheet.

That was when he moved.

Grabbed the terrycloth bath sheet before she found it.

His fingers brushed hers. She cried out, swiped the hair from her eyes.

"No," she said, "don't—"

Karim threaded his hands in the rich, wet gold of her hair. Lifted her face to his and took her mouth in a hard, hungry kiss.

It was what he'd wanted to do that first time.

Then, he'd been able to stop.

No way could he stop now.

She struggled.

He persisted.

And the kiss changed.

It took all his determination to gentle it into something soft and seductive.

His lips moved gently over hers; he whispered her name, whispered how much he wanted her, first in his own language and then in hers.

Everything within him slowed. He wanted the kiss to last forever…

She stopped struggling. She sighed. Her lips clung to his. Her hands rose, touched his chest.

He could feel her trembling, but not with fear.

He felt his blood roar. Felt the earth tilt.

Now, everything in him said, *take her now…*

Karim shuddered.

Then he lifted his head, wrapped the towel around her and got the hell out of the bathroom, out of the apartment, out of the honeyed trap that had surely been set by his brother's clever, beautiful mistress.

CHAPTER FOUR

RACHEL stood where he'd left her, clutching the bath sheet as if it could shield her from him.

Too late, her body hummed, *much too late.*

He'd already done what he'd wanted. Touched her. Kissed her. Taken her on an emotional rollercoaster ride that had taken her from terror to—to—

She jumped at the sound of the front door slamming.

He was gone.

Gasping for air, trembling, she sank down on the closed toilet.

Her brain seemed to be in free-fall. She couldn't think, couldn't make sense of anything.

What had just happened?

Maybe the better question was, what hadn't happened?

The Sheikh had forced himself on her.

He'd walked in while she was naked, drawn her against him, kissed her...

And then he'd let her go.

Why?

Rachel shuddered.

He could have done anything he'd wanted. There'd been nobody to stop him. Certainly not her. He was too big, too strong, that hard body, those sculpted muscles hidden beneath the expensive suit.

She'd have fought him but he'd easily have overpowered her...

A moan broke from her throat.

He *had* overpowered her.

Not just physically.

Mentally.

How else to explain that infinitesimal moment when his mouth had gentled on hers, when his touch had eased and she—and she—

Rachel swallowed dryly.

Never mind that.

His actions had all been deliberate. Terrifying her with a display of strength, the old I-am-Tarzan-you-are-Jane thing.

She knew how that went.

It was a typical male ploy.

The men she dealt with when she waited tables. The ones who were her bosses now in the casino. The players. They were the worst of all. They tossed around their money, showed off their power, stank of cologne...

He hadn't.

Karim.

The Sheikh. The Prince. Whatever he liked to call himself.

No cologne on him. Just the clean scent of himself. The hot scent of a man who wanted a woman

And yet he'd let her go.

Rami would not have done that.

She'd always sensed it in him, the need to dominate, to take what he wanted and to hell with anyone else...

Rachel thrust her fingers into her wet hair and drove it back from her face.

She wasn't dealing with Rami; she was dealing with his brother—and now that she'd had a minute to think, she could see that the brother was a much more wily adversary.

She understood what he'd done. Taken her in a deep, hard kiss and then suddenly turned it into something that was soft, seductive and almost tender.

He'd wanted to confuse her. And he had. That last instant when he'd been kissing her, when she—when she'd had some kind of response to the feel of his mouth on hers...

No. *No!*

Rachel took a deep breath.

She hadn't responded. Not the way he'd wanted. Her reaction had been intuitive. Instinctive. Whatever you wanted to call it.

The I-can-survive-anything woman who lived inside her had taken her straight to automatic pilot.

Let the kiss happen. Stop struggling. That was all she'd done.

She wasn't like Suki.

Money, power, good looks didn't turn her on.

Rachel rose to her feet. She felt better. In fact, she felt fine. Strong. In control.

She even had a plan. Well, a plan of sorts.

And she was wasting precious time, dissecting the ugly little scene as if it mattered when she knew that it didn't.

Karim, the Sheikh of All he Surveyed, would be back.

She didn't have any doubt about it.

Her make-up bag was on a shelf over the sink. Quickly, she opened it, opened the tiny medicine cabinet, swept lipsticks, mascara, eyeliner, aspirin, everything that was there straight inside.

Of course he'd be back, she thought as she pulled a comb through her hair, then secured it in a ponytail.

The man was a lot of things but he was far from stupid.

She knew that he'd seen straight through her lies. Not the one she'd acted out, as if she'd kissed him back when she damned well hadn't.

The other lie. The bigger one.

Not admitting that Ethan was his brother's child.

He knew that he was.

She'd seen it in his cold-as-ice eyes. He didn't have proof yet. That was the only reason he hadn't pushed the conversation further—but he knew.

What he didn't know, couldn't possibly know and absolutely must never know, was that Ethan was not hers.

On the face of it—with Suki gone who knew where and Rami dead—she had as much of a claim to the baby as the Sheikh.

She was his aunt.

He was his uncle.

It should have been a draw—but it wasn't. He had unimaginable wealth. She worried about next month's rent. He had power over a kingdom. She had the power to choose which shift she worked at the casino.

Rachel hurried into the bedroom, pulled open dresser drawers, yanked on a bra and panties, T-shirt, jeans, socks and sneakers.

She had to get out of town, and fast.

The baby was still sleeping. Thank God for small favors. She'd let him sleep until she was ready to leave…

Her breath caught.

The door. The front door. Maybe the Sheikh had only slammed it shut to fool her. Maybe he was still here. And even if he'd left, so what?

He had that damned key.

She flew through the tiny apartment, breathed a sigh of relief when she saw that the living room was empty, secured the lock, grabbed a wooden chair from beside a rickety table and jammed it under the knob.

Let him try and get past that.

A sheikh. A prince. An egotistical anachronism who

thought the world had stood still for the last few hundred years and that he could do anything he wanted.

Anything.

Like take her baby.

"Wrong," Rachel said aloud as she went back to Ethan. "Wrong, wrong, wrong. Dead wrong."

The baby was hers.

Nobody was going to take him from her.

By now, Ethan was awake and fretful. He'd been out of sorts lately; there was a tiny pale spot visible in his pink gums where he was cutting his very first tooth.

Ordinarily she'd have taken him in her arms, settled into the old rocker she'd bought at a Goodwill thrift shop and talked to him—he liked being talked to—but time was a priority now.

"Hey, little man," she cooed as she leaned over the crib, "guess what we're going to do?"

The look he gave her—mouth down-curved, eyes scrunched—said that he didn't much care. Rachel plucked a soft plastic teething ring from the foot of the crib and held it out. The baby's plump fingers closed around the ring and brought it to his mouth.

Good.

She'd bought a few minutes of peace. That was all she needed.

Her suitcase was in the rear of the closet. She took the case out, tossed it on the bed and unzipped it.

Okay.

She packed another pair of jeans. A handful of Ts. Bras. Panties. Socks. A sweater. A zippered hoodie. It all went into the suitcase.

"Ta-da," she told Ethan, still chomping on the brightly colored teething ring. "See how quick that was? Now it's your turn. Any thoughts about what you feel like wearing for our trip? You mean I didn't tell you the surprise? We're going traveling. Doesn't that sound exciting?"

The baby made a rude sound.

"Okay. Maybe not." Rachel pulled open the drawers that held Ethan's clothes. Sleepers. Onesies. Socks. Tiny shirts and sweaters, a pair of grown-up-looking overalls she hadn't been able to resist. "I admit I used to hate it when Mama told me we were going on a trip. She'd take us out of school, Suki and me, just when we'd finally settled in." What else? Diapers, of course. A couple of crib blankets. "Well, I'll never do that to you, little guy. I promise." What was she forgetting? Ah. Formula. Bottles. Little jars of strained fruits and veggies. A quick detour to the kitchen, then back to the bedroom. "I'll find us a place where we can settle down and have a garden and maybe even a kitten."

Rachel paused.

Was that even anywhere near true?

Her mother had run from bill collectors and scandal, but somehow or other those things had always managed to find her anyway.

This was different.

She was running from a prince with the resources of the world at his fingertips.

Rachel shuddered. She wasn't going to think about that now.

Other things were more vital.

Should she head for the airport and blow a stack of cash on a plane ticket, or head for the bus terminal and the first bus out of town?

No contest.

The airport.

She could get away faster and farther, and speed and distance were of paramount importance.

She'd put half her money on a ticket to wherever, half in

reserve for when she and Ethan got there. She had a credit card, too. It was pristine; she'd kept it for emergencies and if this wasn't an emergency, what was?

She'd go as far from Vegas and Rami's brother as that combination of cash and credit would take her. San Francisco, maybe. Or Biloxi, where there were riverboat casinos.

Then she'd get a room, a cheap one, and give herself a couple of days to figure out her next step.

"Ffft," Ethan said.

It made her laugh. Her baby could always do that; he was the one bit of joy she could count on.

"Well, maybe," she said, "but at least it's a plan."

Not much of a plan, but it was a start.

Suki had always teased her about what she'd called "Rachel's obsession with planning" but without some kind of blueprint you could end up like Mama or Suki or half the women in this town.

And that—being kept, living on a man's largesse, being a...a possession—was never, ever going to happen to her.

As for leaving Las Vegas...

She was ready. More than ready.

Vegas had never been more than a stop on the road to something better. She'd only come here after Suki had called, babbling with excitement as she told her that two of the casinos were hiring new dealers.

"It's a great job," Suki had said. "They'll train you and then you can make a lot of money."

Maybe once. Not anymore. The economy was in the toilet. The need for new dealers had gone with it. Rachel had ended up waiting tables, then working the room at the casino—and wondering how she could have been so stupid as to have listened to her sister.

For one thing, if anybody had been hiring dealers why hadn't Suki applied?

For another, Suki hadn't bothered mentioning that she was living week-to-week in a furnished room.

The real reason she'd wanted Rachel to come west was because she'd known Rachel would be resourceful, find a job and an apartment, and she could move in.

She hadn't even asked if her boyfriend, Rami al Safir, could move in, too. He'd just strolled out of Suki's room one morning and after that he had become pretty much a permanent fixture.

A non-bill-paying fixture.

"Fool," Rachel muttered.

But then, she reminded herself as she stuffed a few diapers, a box of baby wipes and some plastic Baggies into a tote, if she hadn't come to Las Vegas she wouldn't have Ethan.

The baby gave a pathetic little sob. He'd lost his teething ring through the bars of the crib. Rachel picked it up, wiped it off and gave it back to him.

He flashed a happy smile.

"Yes," Rachel said, "you're right. This is a fresh start for us both."

A new town. A new place to live. A job that wouldn't put her in costumes that made men see her as an item they could purchase.

A fresh start. Definitely. And all because of a man who thought his money, his titles, his gorgeous good looks—because, yes, he was good-looking, if you liked the type and she certainly didn't—all because of his Sheikhiness, the Prince.

The baby blew a loud, wet bubble. Rachel grinned.

"My very thought," she said.

Okay. Diapers? Check. Formula? Check. A few tiny jars of baby food? A bottle in a small insulted bag? Double check.

And that was it.

Goodbye, Sheikh Karim.

Hello, brand-new life.

Rachel scooped Ethan up and bundled him in a crib blanket printed with prancing blue giraffes. Then, the baby in the curve of one arm, her purse over that shoulder, the diaper bag over the other, she hoisted the suitcase from the bed and walked briskly through the apartment to the front door, shoved the chair out from under the knob, undid the locks and without a single backward glance headed down the stairs.

She was happy to be leaving Las Vegas. She'd been planning on it, only waiting to save a little more money, but what had happened this morning made that irrelevant.

Rachel paused on the ground floor landing.

Dammit. The taxi. She'd neglected to phone for one. And she hadn't called Mrs. Grey to say she wouldn't be needing her to babysit anymore.

No problem.

She could do both things as soon as she got outside and dug her cell phone from her purse.

Wrong.

She couldn't dig out her phone, or call Mrs. Grey, or phone for a taxi.

She couldn't do anything because when she opened the door to the street the first thing she saw was a shiny black car at the curb, its rear door open.

The second thing was the Sheikh, leaning against the fender, arms folded, eyes narrowed, mouth set in a thin line.

Rachel stopped dead. "You," she said.

It was a painfully clichéd reaction and she knew it.

He seemed to think so, too, because a smile knifed across his lips.

"Me," he said, in a voice that reminded her of steel swathed in silk. His gaze dropped to her suitcase. "Going somewhere?"

She felt her face heat. "Get out of my way."

He smiled again, moved toward her, took the suitcase

from her suddenly nerveless fingers, the diaper bag from her shoulder, and dumped them into the back of the car.

That was when she saw the baby seat.

Her stomach dropped.

"If you think—"

"Put the boy in the seat, Rachel."

"How did you—?"

He gave a negligent shrug. "A cell phone and a title can do wonders," he said dryly. "Go on. Put him in the seat."

"You're crazy if you think you're going to take him from me!"

"He is Rami's," Karim said coldly

"He is mine!"

"And that is the only reason I've decided to take you with me."

She blinked. "Take me with you where?"

"There are details to arrange." A faint look of distaste passed over his face. "And I have no intention of dealing with them in this place."

"I don't—I don't know what you're talking ab—"

"Oh, for God's sake, woman." Karim stalked toward her. He stopped inches away, towering over her, his face stern, hard as granite. "Don't play dumb. It doesn't become you. I want my brother's child. You'll want recompense." He paused. "Unless you're willing to give him to me right now."

Rachel stood as straight and tall as she could. For the first time in her life she wished she were wearing those damned stiletto heels.

"If you think I'd ever do that—"

"No. I didn't think it, but then, anything is possible."

"What's possible," she said, "is that I'll scream for help. There are laws in this country—"

"Laws against an uncle wishing to see to the welfare of his dead brother's child? I think not."

"You don't give a damn for Ethan's welfare! You just want to steal my baby, take him far away and bring him up to be—to be a clone of you!"

Karim laughed. She felt a rush of fury sweep through her.

"You're a despicable person!"

"Shall we deal with this in a civilized manner or not?"

Rachel stared up into that beautiful, emotionless face. Then she brushed past him, buckled Ethan into the baby seat and started to get into the car beside him.

The Sheikh closed his hand tightly around her elbow and drew her onto the sidewalk.

"You will sit in the passenger seat," he snapped, "next to me. I am not your chauffeur."

Rachel glared at him.

"You are not anything honest or decent," she said.

It wasn't much of a line, but at the moment it was all she had.

CHAPTER FIVE

WHERE was Karim taking her?

When she'd asked, he'd avoided a direct answer.

Why ask again and give him the pleasure of acknowledging that he was in charge? Maybe thinking that way was foolish but it was the way Rachel felt.

He'd done everything he could to humiliate her. The way he looked at her, talked to her, snapped orders at her...

The way he'd kissed her.

No. She wasn't going to add to it by pleading for information.

She looked back at Ethan and came as close to a smile as she could. Her boy was content; he loved car rides. She had a beat-up old Ford. It wasn't much to look at but it was fairly reliable.

Early on, when Ethan was colicky and crying, and Suki would cover her ears and say, *"Can't that baby ever be quiet?"* Rachel had discovered that taking him for a ride into the desert, sometimes as far as Red Rock Canyon, almost always turned those heartbreaking sobs to gurgles of contentment.

If only she and her baby were alone and heading for the peaceful canyon now, she thought, folding her hands tightly in her lap and staring out the window.

Rachel glanced at the Sheikh.

He drove quickly and competently, his left hand on the steering wheel, his right resting lightly on the gear shifter. His profile was unalterably stern.

The logical destination would be a lawyer's office, but she dismissed that as soon as she thought of it.

Snapping his fingers and making a car seat materialize in the middle of the desert was one thing.

Conjuring up an attorney he'd trust to sort out all the legalese of Ethan's custody was another.

Was he heading for a lab for a DNA test?

No. She doubted that, too.

The Sheikh was accustomed to using his power and money to get what he wanted, but even he had to know that he'd need her consent to get a sample of Ethan's DNA.

After all, she was his mother.

Rachel swallowed hard.

He'd accepted her in that role without hesitation; clearly he didn't know a thing about Suki or the months his brother had spent with her.

And she had every intention of keeping it that way.

Then, where were they going?

To the Strip. That had to be the answer.

It was not terribly far from the grimy building she lived in to the glitzy hotels on the Strip, but you measured the distance in money, not in miles.

That had to be where he was taking her. A restaurant. A coffee shop. Or his suite.

A man like him, a sheikh, would surely have a suite, an enormous, glamorous set of rooms reserved for the rich and famous.

She'd demand they stay in the suite's sitting room and that he leave the door open, though she suspected he would not repeat that kiss.

She was certain she'd figured right, that the kiss had been

a mark of male dominance. Like an alpha wolf marking the boundaries of his turf by peeing on rocks and trees, she thought.

The image made her want to laugh.

But she didn't.

There was nothing funny in being dragged off by a man who thought he owned the world and everyone in it.

The car flew past Circus Circus, past the Venetian, past the Flamingo.

Rachel swung toward her abductor. To hell with not asking him where they were going. He was using mental and emotional muscle to get what he wanted. It was what he excelled at.

The thing she had to do was fight it.

"I want to know where you're taking me."

"I told you," he said calmly. "Somewhere quiet, where we can discuss our situation."

"Our situation?" Rachel snorted. "We have no situation."

Ahead, a traffic light glowed crimson. Karim slowed the car, brought it to a stop.

"You would be wise," he said softly, "not to take me for a fool."

"I asked you a simple question. Surely you can give me a simple answer. Where are we—?"

The light turned green. He made a turn. They were heading away from the Strip, away from the hotels.

A lump of fear lodged in her throat.

The only thing that could possibly draw a visitor to this part of town was the airport.

"Either you tell me where you're going or—"

"We're going to my plane."

Full-blown panic flooded through her.

"I am not getting on a plane!"

"Yes," he said in a quiet voice that resonated with command, "you are."

"No!"

"We're flying to New York."

"*You're* flying to New York! I'm going home."

"Home?" His tone changed, became hard. "Really? Is that why you came out the door with a suitcase?" There was a gate ahead; he slowed the car as they approached it. "I told you not to take me for a fool, Rachel. When you came down those steps your only thought was to run. I'd bet you didn't even have a destination. Well, now you do."

"Get this through your head, Your Highness. There's not a way in hell I'm flying to New York or anyplace else with you. If you think you can—you can pick up where you left off in my apartment—"

He looked at her, his eyes cold. Then he swung the wheel to the right and pulled onto the shoulder of the road.

"I assure you, Ms. Donnelly, I'm not the least bit interested in you sexually."

"If that's your idea of an apology—"

"It's a statement of fact. What happened earlier was a mistake."

"You're damned right it was. And if you think it could ever happen again—"

"I'm taking you to New York so we can move to the end of this little drama as quickly as possible."

"We can do that right here."

"No, we cannot. I have a home in Manhattan. Commitments to keep."

"I have commitments, too."

He laughed. She felt her face heat.

"I'm sure my life doesn't seem anywhere near as important as yours," she said coldly, "but it is to my baby and me."

"I'll have the DNA of the child tested."

His tone was flat. Matter-of-fact, as if the issue had been decided.

That frightened her more than anything else. His certainty that there would be a test. That whatever he demanded would happen.

She knew she had to sound decisive, even in the face of his determination.

"The name of the person who fathered my child is my affair."

"Not if that person was my brother."

His answer was so logical that for a couple of seconds her mind went blank. What could she say to that?

"Why, Rachel," he said softly, "don't tell me you've run out of arguments."

"Here's the bottom line, Your Highness. There won't be a test. I won't grant permission. And there's not a thing you can do about it."

"You're correct," he said quietly. "I can't force you."

Rachel wanted to cheer. Instead, she folded her arms and waited. She knew it couldn't be this easy.

"You may, indeed, refuse my request. You have that right." He smiled. It was a terrible smile; it chilled her to the bone. "But I, too, have rights. Don't bother telling me I don't. I've already spoken with my attorney."

"You've had a busy morning," she said, trying to sound glib despite the race of her heart.

"I have reasonable grounds to think Rami is the child's father."

"So you say."

"So my lawyer will say. If you refuse to have him tested, I'll put this in the hands of the judicial system." He paused. "It is, my attorney says, a very slow-moving system. Who knows how long Ethan will be in foster care?"

Rachel blanched. "No! You can't—"

"Certainly I can," he said calmly. "I have one of the best legal firms in the United States on retainer. Six full partners. Endless associates from the nation's top law schools. Paralegals. Clerks. Offices on both coasts. And who will represent you? A fresh-out-of-law-school kid from Legal Aid? A lawyer with a closet for an office?" Another cool smile touched his lips. "The contest should prove interesting."

It was a direct hit.

Karim knew it; the proof was in the sudden tremor of Rachel Donnelly's mouth, the glitter of unshed tears in her eyes.

He wanted to feel triumphant.

But he didn't.

She was an easy opponent and he'd never been a man who enjoyed easy victories. The power was all his; she had nothing but possession of Rami's son—because, without question, this *was* Rami's son.

Why wouldn't she admit it?

She had everything to gain. She had to know he'd pay whatever price she set for the child.

Unless the child really mattered to her.

He supposed that was possible. Not likely, in his experience. His mother, whenever she'd been around, had shown more affection for her poodles than for him or Rami; he had female employees, executives on the fast track, whose kids were virtually being raised by nannies.

Nothing wrong with that.

It did children good to grow up with a sense of independence.

Wasn't he living proof of that?

Still, he knew there were other kinds of mothers.

He saw them on weekends when he ran in Central Park, playing and laughing with their children

Maybe Rachel had that kind of thing in her.

Maybe not.

Maybe it was all an act.

Either way, he didn't give a damn.

Whatever her reason for making this so complicated, he would be the victor. How much she gained from the battle— six figures, seven, the right to visit with the boy from time to time if she wished—depended on how many obstacles she put in his way.

He really didn't want a court fight.

He knew damned well it would end up splashed in the tabloids, on the cable talk shows, on internet blogs. And both he and Alcantar were better off without that kind of publicity.

Rachel would acquiesce before things went public. He was certain of it. And this, her silence, was the first proof.

So he waited, watching her without saying a word, until at last she blinked back those unshed tears.

"Why are you doing this to me?"

Her voice was whisper-thin. It almost made him feel guilty—until he thought about his duty to his brother.

"This isn't about you," he said, not unkindly. "It's about Rami."

Rachel shook her head. "I don't believe that."

Karim narrowed his eyes.

"No one calls me a liar."

"Not even when you lie to yourself?"

"I have no idea what you're talking about."

"I'm talking about too little, too late." Her voice took on strength; she folded her arms in what was fast-becoming a familiar indication of defiance. "Because, Your Highness, if you'd really cared about your brother you'd have been there for him. You'd have made him see that he couldn't go on drinking and gambling and living the kind of life people like you live, neck-deep in self-indulgence and money and to hell with decency and honor and—"

She gasped as he reached for her, ignoring the pull of his seat belt and hers, digging his hands into her shoulders as he pulled her toward him.

"You don't know a damned thing about what you call 'people like me,' and you sure as hell don't know anything about my brother except what he showed you when he took you to bed."

"I know that you're heartless. To do what you're doing to Ethan and me and, yes, even to your brother's memory—"

"I'm doing this *for* his memory. For the honor of our people—an honor he never understood."

His hands bit into her shoulders. Then he said something under his breath in a language that sounded as hard and unyielding as he was, and flung her from him.

"Agree to the testing or find yourself a way to fight me in court," he growled as he started the car. "Those are your choices. The flight east is a long one. I suggest you use the time to come to a decision."

They stopped at the security gate. Karim produced his ID; the guard waved them through. Rachel waited until he'd parked. Then she turned toward him.

"I just want to get one thing straight." Her voice shook; she cleared her throat, sat straighter, reminded herself that her enemy would surely make the most of any sign of weakness. "You remember that—that moment in the bathroom when—when I seemed to stop fighting you?"

"No," he said coldly, "not in any detail. Did you think I would?"

She felt her face heat but she'd gone too far to back off now.

"You'd have remembered my knee where it would have done the most good if you hadn't let go of me."

"So that was… What shall I call it? Misdirection?"

"It was doing whatever I had to do to get you off me!"

He nodded, his expression suddenly grave. "I'll keep that in mind for next time."

"Believe me, Your Highness, there won't be a next time."

He gave her a long, steady look. Was he laughing at her? Did he think this was a joke?

Rachel didn't wait to find out.

Instead, she undid her seat belt, got out of the car and took Ethan from the baby seat. Karim reached past her, grabbed her suitcase and the diaper bag, then clasped her elbow with his free hand and began walking toward a silver jet with the emblem of a falcon on its fuselage.

Steps led up to the open cabin door where two men and a woman, all in dark gray suits, stood watching them.

"My crew," Karim said.

His crew.

His plane.

His life.

The sudden reality of what was happening hit Rachel with breath-stealing force. She stumbled; Karim dropped the bags and swept his arm around her waist.

"Dammit," he growled.

The woman rushed down the steps and hurried toward them. She reached for the suitcase and diaper bag but Karim shook his head.

"Take the child."

Rachel pulled back. The woman smiled reassuringly.

"He'll be fine with me, ma'am. I'll take him to the galley. I have diapers ready, food, a little carrier... His Highness saw to everything."

Rachel blinked. "He did?"

"He did," Karim said briskly. "Go on. Give the baby to Moira, or would you rather run the risk of dropping him?"

Rachel handed Ethan over. Then she stared at the Sheikh. "When did you order all those things?"

"I had plenty of time to make phone calls while you were packing. There isn't a woman alive who doesn't take forever to pack."

"I didn't take forever. And are you always so sure of how things will work out? That I was packing at all? Just because you want something doesn't mean it—" She gasped as he swung her up in his arms. "I can walk!"

"Yes. So you just demonstrated."

He strode to the steps and climbed them. The two men— his pilots, she assumed—snapped to attention.

Rachel could feel her face burning. Maybe the Sheikh's crew was accustomed to seeing their lord and master board his plane with a woman in his arms but this kind of dramatic entrance was new to her.

"I'll see to those bags, sir," one of the men said.

The Sheikh nodded.

"Fine. I want to get airborne ASAP."

"Yes sir."

One man went for the bags. The other made his way to the cockpit. Karim carried Rachel through what might easily have passed as someone's handsome living room.

"Don't they click their heels?" she said.

He raised an eyebrow. "Excuse me?"

She pulled back as far as she could in his hard, encircling arms.

"I said, don't they click their heels?"

"They do," he said, "but only on state occasions."

Her eyes went to his. Okay. It was a joke; she could tell by the look on his face. At least there was something human about him.

"You can put me down now."

"Can I?"

"Put-me-down!"

His mouth twitched. "I heard you."

"Then, dammit, put me—"

"That isn't a very ladylike way of speaking."

"I'm not a very ladylike lady. And I want you to—"

His arms tightened around her as the plane lifted into the sky.

"I know what you want," he said gruffly, and he bent his head and kissed her.

She made a little sound of protest and he asked himself what in hell he was doing.

And then she made another little sound that had nothing to do with protest.

Karim traced the outline of her lips with the tip of his tongue. He sank onto a leather loveseat, Rachel still in his arms. One hand swept into her hair; the other found the sweet swell of her breast. Her taut nipple pressed into his palm through her cotton T-shirt, and he shuddered.

"Rachel," he whispered.

She moaned and her lips parted, giving him access to the honeyed sweetness of her mouth.

He drew her closer. Swept his hand under her shirt. Cupped her breast.

She put her arms around his neck.

He brought his hand to her face, cupped her jaw, rested his thumb in the delicate hollow of her throat. Her pulse leaped under his touch.

What in hell was he doing?

It was wrong. It was madness. And yet he wanted this, wanted her—

The plane hit an air pocket. It jumped, and so did Rachel. She jerked back in his arms, face pale, eyes wide and blurred. He blinked and let go of her.

She sprang to her feet.

"Do not," she breathed, "do not ever touch me again you—

you vile, arrogant, heartless, manipulative bastard! Do you always ignore the truth of what other people feel?"

She didn't wait for an answer. A good thing, he thought as she stumbled to a seat far from his, because he didn't have one.

Was she right?

Had he ignored what might have been Rami's unspoken cries for help? Could he have saved him from his path of self-destruction? Could he have somehow turned his brother's wasted life around?

And this.

What he'd just done.

Kissing Rachel. Forcing his kisses on her. An ugly way to describe it, but wasn't that what he'd done? Kissed her until she'd kissed him back, until her sighs, the sweetness of her mouth were proof that she was in danger of succumbing to the same hot darkness that threatened him?

Only one thing was certain.

It was too late to do anything about Rami.

But he could do something about the child. Raise him to be the man Rami might have been.

And he could do something about Rami's woman.

He could never touch her again.

Never, Karim told himself, and he turned his face to the window as the plane gained speed and altitude until, at last, the glittering lights far below were no more substantial than a mirage.

CHAPTER SIX

RACHEL was shaking with anger.

Bad enough the Sheikh had walked into her life and seized control of it.

Ordering her around. Making assumptions.

And this. Man-handling her as if—as if she existed for his pleasure.

She knew what he thought of her.

Rami had treated Suki like a slave. *Bring me this, hand me that, don't argue when I say something...*

He'd tried that with her, too, but it hadn't worked.

"Maybe that's how men deal with women where you come from," she'd told him, "but this is America."

America. Where a woman like her wore a costume that made her look like a whore because management said she had to. Where a man judged her by the damned costume, or maybe by the belief that she'd been his brother's mistress.

She'd told him she hadn't been Rami's mistress. He hadn't believed her. Now she wanted to tell him she hadn't been his lover, either.

She wanted to say, *I'd sooner have lived on the streets than have slept with your horrible brother.*

But she couldn't say it. She had to play out this charade because all that mattered was Ethan.

Okay. She had to calm down. Take a deep breath. Let it out slowly. Take another...

"Goddammit," she said.

How could she calm down? How?

"You gotta go with the flow," Mama had always said.

Mama hadn't just gone with the flow, she'd ridden it like a surfer on a wave.

Rachel snorted.

Mama used to say a lot of things. Folksy crap. Stupid nonsense.

Not so stupid anymore.

Go with the flow. And that other old bromide.

"First impressions count."

That had always made Rachel cringe, because Mama had probably said it a hundred times, always in a cheery voice, always as she stood in front of a mirror primping for her first date with the latest jowly, sweaty-faced fool who'd come sniffing at her heels.

Turned out Mama had been right about that, too. First impressions did count. The Sheikh had judged her on how she'd looked. And she'd hadn't helped the situation, letting him bark out commands—

Letting him kiss her in the bathroom and kiss her again, here on his plane. Sure, she'd fought back, but then—but then—

Come on, Rachel. Be honest, at least with yourself.

She'd fought about as hard as a poker player fought against ending up with a Royal Flush.

He'd kissed her.

And after a token kind of resistance she'd kissed him back.

That was the awful truth.

He was every miserable thing a man could be. Too rich, too good-looking, too egotistical to tolerate. Dammit, he was a man, and that was enough.

Until he'd kissed her and her brain had turned to mush.

How could such a thing have happened?

Yes, he was good-looking. Hell, what he was, was sexy.

But she wasn't into sexy.

She wasn't into sex.

She wasn't into anything that might interfere with the life she wanted, the life she'd been planning ever since she woke up in a lumpy bed in a cheap room in Pocatello, Idaho, the morning of her seventeenth birthday. Sixteen-year-old Suki had been asleep next to her, mouth hanging open, each exhalation stinking of beer.

"Mama?" Rachel remembered saying, with a kind of awful premonition.

She'd sat up, pushed away the thin blanket—and had seen the birthday card propped on the table near the bed. A big, garish thing with purple and yellow balloons drawn all over it.

Happy Birthday! it said.

Inside were two crisp twenty dollar bills. And a note.

Gone for a little vacation with Lou! You girls be good until I send for you!
    Luv you!

Lou had been Mama's latest "beau." That was what she always called her men-friends. She'd gone on "little vacations" before. A weekend. A few days. One scary time, when Rachel was ten and Suki was nine, she'd gone off for an entire week.

That morning in Pocatello Rachel had told herself that Mama would be back.

It never happened.

After three weeks she'd found a night job at Walmart but it hadn't been enough to pay for their miserable room and put food in their bellies.

So she'd quit school.

One more year until she'd have had her diploma. It had killed her to walk away, but what choice had there been? She'd had to work to support herself and her sister.

"You stay in school, Suki," she'd told her. "You hear me? One of us in going to graduate!"

In August, Rachel had moved the two of them to a bigger furnished room in a safer neighborhood. She'd used her Walmart discount for Suki's school supplies and bought their clothes at Goodwill.

Suki wouldn't wear them.

"Holy crap, how can you wear somebody's old stuff?" she'd demanded. "And you're wasting your money, buying me school stuff. I'm not going to go no more."

When the first snow fell they got a card from Mama. She was in Hollywood. She knew someone who knew someone who was making a movie. She was going to get a part in it.

And then I'll send for my girls!

More exclamation marks. More lies. They'd never heard from her again.

Or maybe they had. There was no way to know because by January Idaho was nothing but a memory.

Suki had taken off. No goodbyes, no explanations. Just a note.

See you, it said.

Just like Mama, except Mama had left those twenties. Suki had emptied the sugar bowl of the fifty bucks Rachel had kept in it.

Rachel moved to Bismarck, North Dakota. Took a job as a waitress. Moved to Minneapolis. Took another job waitressing. A couple more stops and she'd ended up in a Little Rock, Arkansas, diner.

Bad food, grungy customers, lousy tips.

"There's got to be somewhere better than this," she'd muttered one night, after a guy walked out without paying his bill, much less leaving a tip.

"Dallas is lots better," the other girl working the night shift had said.

Right, Rachel thought now, swallowing a bitter laugh. And after Dallas came Albuquerque, and after that Phoenix.

Rachel had seen more than her share of the West.

Then Suki had called. Told her about Las Vegas.

In some ways Vegas had been an improvement. When customers were happy because they'd won at the slots they left decent tips. And once she'd swallowed her pride and taken the job she had now the tips had got even better.

She'd started taking classes at the university, planned a better life for herself, and then for herself and Ethan...

What time was it, anyway?

She wasn't sure what time they'd left Las Vegas. Ten, eleven o'clock—something around there. They were moving fast but there was no feeling of motion, no sense that they were miles above the earth, going from one time zone to another.

Could that be disorienting? Could it explain...

No. There'd been no plane, no soaring through the sky that first time the Sheikh had kissed her.

Nothing but the man himself. The taste of him. The feel of him. The heat and hardness of his body.

It didn't make sense. She wasn't like that. She wasn't into what Suki called "hooking up."

It drove Suki crazy

"My sister, the saint," she'd sneered when Rachel had caught her drinking Southern Comfort after she knew she was pregnant. "Such a good girl. Always flosses. Always eats her veggies. Never gets laid."

Rachel had snatched the bottle from Suki's hand and dumped the whiskey into the sink.

"A little screwing would make you more human," Suki had yelled after her.

No, Rachel had thought, it wouldn't. It would just mark her as her mother's daughter.

Sex had been her mother's addiction. Her sister's.

Not hers.

Sex was a trap. It robbed you of common sense, and for what? A few minutes of pleasure, or so she'd heard women say. She had no idea if that was true or not. She'd tried being with a man once or twice and all she'd ended up feeling was even more alone.

She didn't need men, didn't need sex, didn't need anything or anyone. Well, except for Ethan. Other than the baby, she was content to be alone.

She was a cool-headed woman who thought things through. A pragmatist. A survivor.

And that was why she'd defeat the Sheikh at this game.

She was not handing control of her life to him.

She was not giving up her baby.

Rachel rose to her feet.

Half a dozen steps took her to the alcove where Ethan slept in his carrier. The flight attendant was sleeping, too; she sensed Rachel's presence and jerked awake.

"What can I get you, miss?" she said quickly. "Something to eat, perhaps? There are sandwiches, fruit, coffee—"

"Nothing, thank you. I just wanted to see how my baby's doing."

"Oh. He's fine. I changed him a while ago, fed him—"

"Yes. That's great. I'm just going to take him back to my seat with me."

Rachel picked up the carrier, took it down the aisle. It was impossible not to see Karim but her gaze swept over him without their eyes making contact.

He didn't even know she was there.

He was talking on his cell phone. She heard a couple of words. "Suite." "Accommodations for an infant." Nothing more than that.

She sat down, put Ethan's carrier on the seat next to hers, took a soft throw blanket from another seat and draped it over her lap.

She was cold. And, yes, she was hungry. But she didn't want the Sheikh's food.

What she wanted was to know his next move.

A stop at a law office or a laboratory, at this hour of the night?

She didn't think so.

She thought about what she'd heard him say. "Suite." "Accommodations for an infant."

He was making hotel arrangements.

A suite for Ethan and her. A gilded cage where he could keep them prisoner while he arranged for that damned DNA test.

Until this minute she hadn't had time to think about the test. Or tests. What would testing involve?

Some of Rami's DNA, obviously. Easy enough to come by a strand of hair, she supposed, for a brother.

What if he wanted a DNA sample from her? She couldn't imagine why he would. He'd never questioned whether or not she was Ethan's mother, but what if he did? She knew little about DNA tests, only what she'd picked up from television and movies. Was her DNA the same as Suki's? Was it at least similar enough to establish the baby as hers?

What if it wasn't?

Bad enough that the test would confirm Rami as his father, but if it didn't confirm her as his mother—

She couldn't wait to find out.

She had to run. She'd failed the first time. But she wouldn't fail again.

She'd be as devious as her enemy.

He was putting her in a hotel. He wouldn't leave her on her own; he'd leave her with watchers. Flunkies to make sure she stayed put like an obedient dog.

Oh, she could read him like a book. But she had the one thing he didn't.

Street-smarts.

If he left a guy in her suite, she'd put on an act of desperation.

I need diapers right away, she'd say. *The baby's made an awful mess!*

That would get her watcher out the door.

And she'd take Ethan and run. Not to the lobby, because the Sheikh might have somebody there, too.

No problem. She'd worked in enough hotels to know there were other ways out. Fire exits. Delivery entrances. Basements.

When the Sheikh came for Ethan and her in the morning, all he'd find was an empty suite. And a note.

For the first time in hours Rachel almost smiled.

Goodbye notes were a Donnelly family tradition.

Several rows back, Karim watched Rachel through narrowed eyes.

He was good at reading body language. Years in the stuffy formality of the palace, followed by years of negotiating multi-million-dollar deals with some of the world's toughest opponents, had given him that ability.

For the past hour he'd been reading hers.

For a long time she'd sat stiffly in her seat, her body almost quivering with anger.

She hated him for that kiss.

At first he'd been a heartbeat away from marching up the aisle, hauling her into his arms and carrying her to the small private bedroom in the rear of the cabin.

Two minutes alone and he'd damned well show her that he had not forced that kiss on her, that whatever dark and dangerous thing was happening between them involved her as much as him.

Thank God, sanity had prevailed.

He'd calmed down. So had she. Her shoulders had relaxed, if only a little, and then she'd gone to collect the child.

He'd watched her come down the aisle again, head up, eyes cold as they raked over his face.

Do not even think of touching me, that look had said, but he wouldn't have anyway.

The sight of the baby had reminded him of what this was about—that taking her to New York had nothing to do with her or him; it had to do with Rami.

If the child was his brother's, then it was also his.

He owed it to the boy.

Maybe he owed it to Rami, too.

What he'd thought about earlier, that maybe, just maybe, he'd missed the opportunity to help his brother turn his life around, had set him thinking.

Doing right by Rami's son would go a long way toward doing right by Rami. It would leave a far better legacy than all those bills and chits.

That it would also strip the Donnelly woman of her son was secondary. The boy would obviously be better off in a new life. He could explain that to her.

If she truly loved the child…

He was a second away from heading up the aisle to try and explain that to her when he noticed that she no longer looked tense.

That was when he knew she was planning something.

So much for explaining anything.

He'd kept her from making a break for freedom. And she was going to try again. Not that her trying to get away made any more sense now than before.

What did she have to gain by running?

And yet, had he not been waiting outside that miserable building in which she lived, she'd have disappeared by now.

Did she figure she could get more money out of him if he had to waste time searching for her?

The truth was, he didn't give a damn what it would cost to gain custody of the boy. He'd threatened her with legal proceedings but going to court would be a last resort. Most of his clients abhorred publicity.

As for the effect back home…

The eyes of the world would fix on the scandal. His father would be devastated.

Karim shut his eyes.

He didn't want to think about it. Not yet. Not until he absolutely had the test results in hand.

Which he would, tomorrow.

He'd made the necessary calls. First he'd phoned the Vegas hotels where Rami had owed money and arranged for payment to them all. With that out of the way, he'd contacted his attorney. His physician. His chief of staff. They were the only people he could trust right now. He'd given instructions to each of them and now all he had to do was make sure the woman didn't slip away with the child.

He still couldn't imagine why she would want to. That was a puzzle, but then, so was she.

She seemed to really care about the boy. That, alone, was hard to comprehend. She was clearly broke, and having a baby to worry about surely only made her financial situation more difficult.

And then there were her other traits.

She was stubborn. Defiant. Outspoken. The worst qualities of modern women, all in one package.

Women, modern or not, should not be like that.

Women were supposed to be…perhaps *compliant* was too strong a word.

He had never dealt with a woman like this before.

"Of course you're right, sir," they'd say in business, because he was, after all, not only a sheikh but head of a multi-billion-dollar investment fund.

If the relationship was intimate, a woman would leave off the "sir", but both he and she knew who was in charge.

His last mistress had been spectacularly beautiful and, supposedly, incredibly intelligent—but she'd never argued with him over anything.

He liked it that way…

Then how come, after a while, he'd had the grim feeling that if he'd said something like, *Alanna, how about walking on coals to amuse me?* she'd have smiled prettily and said, *Just let me get a match.*

He scowled, pushed aside the papers he'd been pretending to read, and folded his arms.

He knew how Rachel would react if he said something like that to her.

Angry as he was—at his brother, at her, at the situation the two of them had left for him to deal with—he wanted to laugh.

She'd begin with *You can go to hell* and work up exponentially from there.

He knew, too, what his response would be.

He'd pull her into his arms, whisper what she could do to please him, and that look of indignation would be replaced by one of hot desire.

She'd rise on her toes and bring her mouth to his and he

would ease her down on his bed, undress her, bare her to his mouth, his hands…

Dammit!

He was hard as a rock.

An intelligent man didn't mix business with pleasure, and this was strictly business.

Yes, she was attractive.

All right.

She was beautiful.

And she surely would know how to pleasure a man.

That was a given.

For one thing, Rami had never been interested in innocence. And then a man had only to see her in that costume to know that, whatever her work might be, she was a sexual sophisticate.

Still, when you came down to it, she was just a woman. Not that he held women in low esteem or anything, but she wasn't special—not to a man who'd always had his pick of them.

His mother's genes, his father's royal lineage, his own success… Add all that together and he'd always had his share of desirable lovers.

More than his share, to be brutally honest.

Then why all this schoolboy nonsense?

Karim frowned.

Because he'd been living like a monk, that was why. He'd been so busy cleaning up after Rami instead of living his own life that he had not been with a woman in weeks.

Well, he'd remedy that soon enough.

Karim glanced at his watch.

They'd be in New York in a couple of hours. His driver would meet them at the airport. It would be early evening by the time they reached his penthouse; he'd given orders to ready one of the guest suites for the woman and the child.

A hot shower. A night's sleep. Then, in the morning, a meeting with his attorney, a stop at the lab his doctor had recommended, a bit of serious negotiating with the woman, and custody would be his.

With any luck at all, this would be settled in a couple of days, after which he'd take out his BlackBerry, choose a name and number, and put an end to these weeks of celibacy.

Talk about tying up loose ends, Karim thought with a tight smile.

That would surely do it.

CHAPTER SEVEN

"Miss?"

Rachel's eyes flew open. The flight attendant smiled at her.

"We'll be landing within the hour. I thought you might have changed your mind about eating something, or that you'd like some coffee or juice while we still have time."

"Coffee would be—" Rachel cleared her throat. "Coffee would be fine, thank you."

"I'll bring it right away."

Rachel nodded. Her throat wasn't the only thing needed clearing. Her brain did, too. She was groggier than before she'd fallen asleep...

Where was Ethan?

Her heart thudded.

He'd been in his carrier, right next to her.

"Moira?"

"Yes, miss?"

"Where's my baby?"

"Oh, I brought him up front with me. He woke up and he seemed hungry—"

Rachel sighed with relief. "Thank you."

"No problem, miss. He's a very sweet little boy."

Rachel smiled. "He's teething, you know, and—"

"I figured as much. I remember my own children at that

age. I chilled one of the teething rings you had in the diaper bag and gave it to him. It seemed to make him happy. He's sound asleep now, though. Why don't I keep him with me? That way, we won't risk waking him and he might sleep through the landing. Descents, the change in pressure, can make some babies uncomfortable."

"Yes. That's fine. Thanks again."

"My pleasure, miss. I'll get that coffee now."

"Black, please."

"Black it is."

Rachel brought her seat upright and looked out the window. Were they as high over the earth as they'd been before? It was hard to tell. The long flight, the change in time zones…all of it was disorienting—though not as disorienting as being plucked out of your own life at the command of a prince.

Was he still seated in the middle of the plane? She wanted to turn around and look but she wouldn't give him the satisfaction.

What was he doing? Was he asleep? Was he working on those papers he'd taken from his attaché case? Was he staring out the window the way she was while he planned his next move?

She could find out.

She didn't have to make a point of looking at him. All she had to do was rise from her seat and walk to the lavatory in the rear of the plane.

She needed to do that, anyway, sheikh or no sheikh.

Quickly, before she could change her mind, Rachel rose to her feet.

He was still seated where he'd been all along. His seat was halfway reclined; he looked completely relaxed, long legs stretched out, big shoulders pressed against the leather seat-back, hands folded loosely in his lap.

And his face...

Her breath caught.

It was an incredible face.

His eyes were shut; his lashes, so thick and dark a woman would kill for them, lay arced against his chiseled cheek-bones. Stubble smudged his jaw.

He was—there was no other word for it—beautiful.

Dark. Sleek. A magnificent predatory animal.

A panther.

His eyes flew open and met hers. His pupils contracted; she saw his mouth thin.

Heat flared in her belly.

She stared at his mouth, remembered the silken feel of it against hers...

Stop it!

She wanted to run, but you didn't try to escape from a panther. You stood your ground.

Head up, eyes straight ahead, she walked briskly past him to the lavatory, shut the door—

And fell back against it, heart at full gallop.

This had to stop.

He was the enemy. He was a very dangerous enemy. There was no reason for her to be attracted to him. She'd never been drawn to bad boys at the age some girls were, and she'd certainly never been drawn to the grown-up version.

Bad boys were Suki territory, not hers.

Okay. A couple of deep breaths. A couple of slow exhalations. Then she stepped away from the door.

The bathroom held a marble sink and vanity, a glass-enclosed shower, a toilet and glass-fronted cabinets neatly stocked with folded towels, packaged soaps, toothbrushes and pretty much everything anyone could want.

Rachel gave the shower a look of longing but, no, she wasn't going to use it. The thought of stripping naked with only the door between the Sheikh and her brought back the memory of what had happened this morning. Or yesterday morning. Or, dammit, whatever day this was and that had been...

What did the day matter?

It was what had happened that counted.

Karim, his eyes going dark as he looked at her naked body. His hands cupping her breasts, his fingers feathering over her suddenly erect nipples, the liquid heat gathering low in her belly...

A moan rose in her throat.

She bit it back and stared at herself in the mirror.

"He caught you by surprise," she said.

Her reflection returned the stare. *Really?* it said in a sly voice. *So what are you saying, hmm? That you've never been caught by surprise before?*

Rachel blinked.

Why was she wasting time and energy over this? What happened next was all that mattered. She had to be prepared to deal with it.

But not looking like this.

Looks were important. Another Mama-ism, like the one about first impressions and, again, true enough. Look weak, people saw you as weak. Look tough, they figured that you were.

Right now, she looked pitiful.

Red-rimmed eyes. The pallor that came of exhaustion. Hair that was half in, half out of a ponytail.

"You," she told her reflection, "look worn and defeated. Is that how you want his Imperial Sheikhiness to see you?"

The answer was obvious.

So she got busy. Used the toilet. Ran water into the sink. Washed her hands and face with a soapy liquid that smelled like lemons. Brushed her teeth. Yanked her hair free of the band that constrained it and then combed it again and again until it was tangle-free.

Then she stood tall and looked into the mirror again.

"Better," she said.

Not much, but anything was an improvement.

A deep breath. A toss of her head. Then she unlocked the door, started up the aisle…

The plane hit an air pocket. Not much of an air pocket, just enough to make her stumble. The problem was that it happened just as she reached the seat where he was sitting.

Not again, she thought as his hand shot out and closed around her wrist.

The panther was wide awake.

His fingers were warm and hard against her skin. Rachel looked at him. He looked at her. *Say something,* she told herself, and she forced a polite smile.

"Thank you."

"Amazing."

"What?"

"That 'thank you.' Surely that's a phrase I never thought to hear you say, *habibi.*"

He was smiling. It wasn't much of a smile, only a tilt of his lips, but it was so private and sexy that, just for an instant, she wanted to smile back.

She didn't, of course. All the sexy smiles in his no doubt considerable repertoire wouldn't be enough to lull her into forgetting who he was and what he wanted.

"I am polite when politeness is appropriate," she said coolly.

This time, he grinned.

"Nicely done. It takes talent to deliver a remark that sounds polite but is really an insult." He tugged on her hand. "Sit down."

"Thank you, but I'm fine."

"Two thank-yous—only one with real validity. Sit down, *please*. Is that better?"

What now? If she refused, would he let go of her, or would he force her to take the seat next to his? Finding out might not be worth what it would cost in terms of losing face over such a stupid game.

Rachel shrugged and slipped into the seat nearest to him.

"Good," he said, and let go of her wrist. "Moira's bringing us coffee. And something to eat."

"She's bringing *me* coffee at my seat. And I'm not hungry."

"Don't be foolish, Rachel. Of course you're hungry. Besides, in my country, refusing to break bread with someone is a discourtesy."

"We're not in your country."

"But we are." The flight attendant came down the aisle, pushing a small wheeled cart laden with trays of fruit, cheese and small sandwiches as well as a silver coffee service.

To her horror, Rachel's belly growled. Karim grinned.

"So much for not being hungry." He waved the attendant away, poured two cups of coffee, then picked up a plate and filled it with tiny sandwiches and fruit. "And so much for not being in my country." He looked at her as he handed her the plate, silverware and an enormous linen napkin. "I am a prince."

"So you've made clear."

"I am my country's diplomat."

"How nice for you," Rachel said sweetly.

"It means that wherever I live is a part of Alcantar." Karim sipped his coffee. "My home in New York. My weekend place in Connecticut." He paused. "This aircraft. When you are in those locations you are subject to the laws of my people. Do you understand?"

"I'm an American citizen. You can't simply—"

"This is not subject to debate. It is fact. When you are on what you Americans would call my turf, the laws of Alcantar apply."

Rachel's hand shook. Carefully, she put down the coffee cup.

"Stop talking in circles," she said flatly. "And stop telling me you can do whatever you wish about Ethan. I'm a citizen. So is he. End of story."

"Perhaps you'd let me finish speaking before you start lecturing me." Karim waited. Then he cleared his throat. "I have been thinking…"

"Am I supposed to be impressed?"

He wanted to laugh. So determined to show no weakness—but he'd noticed how her hand had trembled. She was, indeed, an interesting woman. Tough and tender at the same time. Loving, at least to the child.

Would she be like that in bed?

Dammit, he had to stop his thoughts from wandering.

"We are adults," he said calmly. "And we both want what is best for the boy."

"Ethan, you mean."

"Yes. We want the right thing for him. There's no reason we should be enemies."

"And what is it you see as the right thing, Your Highness?"

"Please. Call me Karim."

What kind of game was this?

Rachel sipped her coffee, hid her confusion in the cup. This was a new approach but she wasn't buying it, not for a second.

Maybe he'd spent the flight reviewing the situation and he'd decided it would be simpler to have her cooperation than to fight for it.

And maybe it took one liar to see through the falsehoods

told by another, because it was painfully obvious that they didn't want the same thing for Ethan at all.

She wanted her baby to be raised with love and warmth.

He wanted him to be raised as Rami's son. And just look at how well that had turned out for Rami, she thought coldly.

"I'm glad we agree on the importance of Ethan's welfare," she said politely. "But—"

"Why did my brother abandon you?"

The question took her by surprise.

"You know, I really don't want to talk about—"

"Why not? I should think you'd have a lot to say about a man who was your lover, who made a child with you and then left you both."

"That's in the past. And—"

"Did he not make any financial arrangements for you and the baby?"

Rachel put down her cup.

"I appreciate your concern, Your Highness, but as I said, that's in the past."

"And this is the future with which my brother should have been concerned. He made no provisions for you or the boy, did he?"

She stared at him. His face was taut with anger. At Rami, she realized, not at her.

It made her feel guilty about the lies she'd told him, the one enormous lie, and wasn't that ridiculous?

"Did he walk out? Did he at least tell you he was leaving?"

Rachel shook her head.

"No," she said softly. That, at least, was true.

There was a silence.

"But he cared for you," Karim finally said.

Rachel didn't answer. A couple of seconds went by. Then he cleared his throat.

"I know it won't change things but you should know that he was not always so—so uncaring. Our childhoods were—difficult. The things we experienced changed him."

"And they didn't change you?"

"I am sure they did, but we chose different ways of dealing with those experiences." A shrug of those wide, masculine shoulders. "Who can explain why one sibling takes one approach to life and the other—"

"No one can explain it," Rachel heard herself say.

"That's kind of you, but—"

"It isn't kind at all. It's just a fact. I have—I have a sister. And—and I have better memories of her when we were little than I do of the years after."

Karim nodded. "She is not like you," he said quietly.

"No. We've always been very different."

"And she would not fight me to keep her child, as you surely will, even though I will raise him as a prince."

"No," Rachel said quickly, "I don't care that he's a prince. He's—he's—"

She clamped her lips together, but it was too late.

Karim's eyes were dark and unreadable, but there was a harshness in his voice that hadn't been there a moment ago.

"It is too late to deny it, Rachel. The boy is Rami's."

She stared at him. That was what this had been about. It hadn't been a peace offering. It had been a clever way of getting her to confess that Rami had fathered her baby.

What a fool she'd been to think this man might truly have a heart, or to forget that he was the enemy.

Rachel put her cup and plate on the cart.

"You keep missing the one thing that matters," she said coldly. "Ethan is mine."

"He is a prince."

"He is a little boy. And he has a name."

"What has that to do with anything?"

"You never use his name. You speak of him as if he were a—a thing. A commodity."

Karim dumped his plate on the cart and shoved the cart away.

"This is ridiculous! Will it make you happy if I call him by the name my brother chose for him? Fine. I'll do that. I'll call him—"

Rachel shot to her feet.

"Your brother didn't name Ethan. I did."

Karim rose, too. If only he didn't tower over her. She hated having to look up at him, to give him that seeming authority over her.

"In that case," Karim said stiffly, "I apologize for him yet again. Apparently, he ignored all his responsibilities."

"Dammit, stop apologizing for him!"

"It is my duty. I understand that he hurt you, but—"

"Hurt me?" Rachel slapped her hands on her hips. "I hated your brother!"

"And yet," Karim said coldly, "you slept with him."

Her cheeks heated.

"You let him put a child in your womb."

She turned away from him and started up the aisle. Karim went after her, caught her by the shoulder and swung her toward him.

"What kind of woman are you? You hated him. But you slept with him. You let him give you a child."

Her mouth trembled. If ever she'd wanted to tell the truth, it was now. But she couldn't, couldn't, couldn't—

"Things—things happen," she said, knowing just how ugly the answer sounded.

Karim's mouth twisted with distaste.

"Is that what you say when you give yourself to a man? That *things happen*?"

"It wasn't—it wasn't the way you make it sound."

"I'll bet it wasn't." He caught her chin, forced her to look into his eyes. "Was he flush with winnings when he first bedded you?"

Rachel's hand shot up. He caught it, caught both her wrists and imprisoned them against his chest.

"How much did you cost him? How much did it take to overcome your hatred, *habibi*?"

"You bastard! You miserable bastard! You don't know anything about me. Not a damned thing—do you understand? Not one single damned—"

His mouth closed over hers.

She fought him. Struggled. And then, as before, the earth tilted beneath her feet and her mind emptied of everything but the taste of him, the feel of him, the way his arms closed around her.

He lifted her off the floor, his mouth angling over hers, plundering hers, and she tunneled her fingers into his hair as he drew her hard against him.

"I hate you," she whispered against his mouth even as she kissed him, even as she gasped at the feel of his hands cupping her bottom. "I hate you, Karim, I hate you…"

A bell rang. It rang again, and then the pilot's disembodied voice announced that they'd be landing in five minutes.

Karim set her on her feet. His face was all planes and angles; his eyes were dark.

Her own eyes stung with tears.

"If you ever do anything like that again…" she said, and then she clamped her lips together.

She was as much to blame as he. He'd started the kiss but she had fallen into it.

Tears of rage stung her eyes. At him? At herself? It didn't matter. This wouldn't happen again.

She wouldn't let it.

She spun away, took a seat and belted herself in. The

wheels kissed the runway. As soon as the plane came to a stop she undid her seat belt and got to her feet, but not in time to prevent the Sheikh from clasping her shoulder and pulling her to him.

"Welcome to New York, *habibi*," he growled. "And do not make promises you won't be able to keep."

He bent his head to hers. Captured her mouth. She groaned, felt her body flush with heat…

And she bit him.

Bit his bottom lip hard enough to make him jerk back and let her go.

A spot of crimson bloomed against his flesh. He touched his finger to it, looked at her, and then his eyes narrowed.

"If you want to play games," he said softly, "I'll be happy to accommodate you."

She wanted to respond, to make some clever remark, but her brain refused to function.

Karim kept his eyes on hers as he lowered his head again, kissed her again, a slow, lingering kiss. She tasted the salt of his blood, the heat of his hunger. She wanted to tear her lips from his but she didn't, she didn't—

He raised his head, looked into her flushed face with a hot glint of triumph in his eyes.

Then he brushed past her on his way to the exit door.

A chauffeured black Mercedes was waiting for them.

The driver held the door open.

The interior of the car was handsome and urbane—except for the baby seat.

The man had thought of everything.

How far was it to the hotel?

Rachel was exhausted, as desperate for sleep as she'd ever been in her life. She needed a long, hot shower, some sleep and then—

2 Free Books!

If you have enjoyed reading this book... [illegible faded text]

As a member of the Mills & Boon Book Club you'll receive all these exclusive benefits:

- 🌹 FREE Home Delivery
- 🌹 Receive new titles TWO MONTHS AHEAD of the shops
- 🌹 Exclusive Special Offers & Monthly Newsletter
- 🌹 Special Rewards Programme

We hope that after receiving your free books you'll want to remain a member. But the choice is yours. So why not give us a go? You'll be glad you did!

For all the latest news and offers, why not visit
millsandboon.co.uk

Mrs/Miss/Ms/Mr .... Initials ....
BLOCK CAPITALS PLEASE

Surname ....

Address ....

....

....

.... Postcode ....

Email ....

P2CIA

NO STAMP
NEEDED!

MILLS
& BOON®
Book Club

FREE BOOK OFFER
FREEPOST NAT 10298
RICHMOND
TW9 1BR

NO STAMP
NECESSARY
IF POSTED IN
THE U.K. OR N.I.

Then, freedom.

The Mercedes merged onto a multi-lane highway. What time was it, anyway? It was too dim in the car to read her watch properly. Did it say four p.m.? That was the time in Nevada, and this was New York, which meant it was—

"It's seven," Karim said. "In the evening."

Rachel looked at him. "Thank you," she said coolly, "but I didn't ask."

"You didn't have to. I know you're probably feeling disoriented."

"Sorry to disappoint you, Your Highness, but I'm not."

"Of course you are."

What would she gain by arguing? Instead, she stared out the window. The ride into the city seemed endless, but finally they were on a wide street, tall buildings on one side, what seemed to be a dense park on the other.

Where was the hotel?

She turned toward him. "How much further to the hotel?"

"What hotel?"

"The one where you're stashing Ethan and me."

He laughed. God, she wanted to slap his face!

The Mercedes pulled to the curb. The door swung open. The hotel, Rachel thought. But the man who bent down and peered into the car wasn't a hotel doorman because what hotel doorman would all but click his heels and say, "Welcome home, Your Highness. I trust you had a good trip."

"Home?" Rachel said. Her voice rose. "Home?"

"My home," Karim said coldly. "My little piece of Alcantar."

Ethan began to wail. Karim reached for him. Rachel tried to stop him. Ethan screamed louder.

"Let go of the boy," Karim said quietly, and, really, what choice was there?

She let go, watched her baby all but disappear in the arms

of the only man she'd ever hated more than she'd hated Rami, more than she'd hated the endless chain of men who had tromped through her mother's life.

The doorman stared at her. Then he held out his hand.

"Miss?"

She slid across the soft leather seat, ignored the extended hand and marched to the lobby door. The doorman rushed by her and managed to open it just as she reached it. She breezed past him, past a high desk with another uniformed flunky seated behind it.

"Miss," he said, as politely as if this kind of circus took place here every day.

Karim was waiting for her, standing beside an elevator with Ethan in his arms.

A smiling, gurgling Ethan.

Traitor, Rachel thought, as she stepped inside the elevator car.

Unless she was willing to walk away from her baby—and that would never happen—she was now, to all intents and purposes, the Sheikh's prisoner.

CHAPTER EIGHT

SOMEWHERE around three in the morning, even New York City finally slept.

Not Karim.

He stood at one of the floor-to-ceiling windows in his darkened bedroom, bare-chested, wearing only gray sweatpants that were a leftover from his days at Yale. Behind him, the rumpled bed offered mute testimony to the hours he'd spent tossing and turning.

Ridiculous.

He should have been exhausted.

He hadn't slept at all last night, and his day had started with the discovery that his brother had a child. Add in his confrontations with Rachel, the five-hour flight from Nevada to New York, the hours spent in his study, trying to catch up with the messages and emails on his cell phone and his computer...

He'd fallen into bed somewhere after midnight. Sleep should have come quickly.

It hadn't.

Instead, he'd envisioned Rachel in a guest suite down the corridor. What was she thinking? What was she doing? Had her anger at him eased or was she still breathing fire as she had hours earlier, when she'd found out he wasn't taking her to a hotel but to his home?

The memory almost made him laugh.

He'd never seen a woman so furious. And she hadn't been shy about letting him know it.

He couldn't think of another woman in his life who'd have objected to spending the night with him—but, of course, she wasn't really spending it with him.

If she were, he wouldn't be asleep now, either. He'd be in his bed with her in his arms…

"Hell!"

Karim strode into his bathroom, turned on the sink faucet, bent his head under the flow of cold water and took a long drink while the water cooled his face. He toweled off with impatient strokes and then went back to the window again.

He was not a man given to erotic imaginings. Why would he be, when there was always a woman eager to offer the real thing?

He wasn't given to insomnia, either, no matter how long or difficult his day had been.

And yet he was standing here, wide awake.

Eighteen stories below, Fifth Avenue was deserted save for an occasional taxi or some unlucky dog owner being pulled along at the end of a leash. Central Park was a hushed dark green jungle on the opposite side of the street. Beyond the park, even the glittering lights of the Manhattan skyline seemed dim.

Wonderful, Karim thought grimly. The entire world was asleep except for him.

He'd never needed much sleep, four or five hours was more than enough, but he wasn't fool enough to think he could get through a day of decision-making without some kind of rest, and tomorrow was going to be a day filled with decision-making.

After speaking with his P.A. he'd set up two meetings: breakfast with a Tokyo banker at the Regency, then midmorning coffee downtown, at Balthazar, with an official from India. At noon, he'd have lunch in the boardroom with his own staff.

He'd been away from his office far too long. He had business to conduct and he also needed to touch base with his people.

And then there was the rest.

Karim's mouth thinned.

At two o'clock he'd meet with his attorney.

He and Rachel.

He knew it would not be easy to negotiate a custodial arrangement with her. She was going to be difficult.

What would it take to get her to give up her rights to the boy? She'd said she never would but that was talk. People always had a price. Women, especially.

Yes, they liked his looks. They liked his virility. But he knew damned well they liked his title and his wealth even more.

That was surely how Rami had caught Rachel's attention. Money, a title…

But Rami hadn't had money. The proof was in that desolate little apartment where he'd lived with her. As for the title… Rachel found titles laughable.

He found that amusing, because he wasn't impressed by them, either. He had, at least, earned his own fortune, but he'd been born to the silly string of honorifics. He hadn't done a thing to earn them but he'd grown accustomed to others not seeing things that same way.

Most people, especially women, heard who he was and began to act as if this was pre-revolutionary France and he was the Sun King. They gushed. They fluttered their lashes. He'd been on the receiving end of more than one curtsy and it always embarrassed the hell out of him when it happened.

The thought of Rachel gushing or fluttering or curtsying was laughable.

She'd made it clear that she was disdainful of his being a prince, a sheikh, heir to the throne of Alcantar. That he was almost embarrassingly rich didn't win any points from her, either.

She treated him the way he suspected she'd treat anybody else. Anybody else she didn't like, he thought, and he smiled.

Rachel was a very interesting woman.

She was a woman making it on her own, with a child to raise. That couldn't be easy. His mother—his and Rami's—had been a woman with all possible means and resources at her fingertips, yet her sons had been amusing at best and at worst an inconvenience.

He could not imagine Rachel ever feeling inconvenienced by the child.

So what?

Good mother or not, the baby would be better off with him. Being a prince was the child's destiny. Rachel would get over losing him…

Dammit, why was he thinking about her at all?

His mouth thinned.

He knew why.

Sex.

He wanted Rachel in his bed.

He wanted her naked and moaning beneath him, wanted the taste of her on his tongue. He wanted her scent on him, her wet heat on him, he wanted to sink into her and watch her eyes blur as he made her come and come and come…

Karim cursed and rubbed his hands over his face. He was being a damned fool.

He'd kissed her but that would not happen again. Absolutely it would not. He certainly would not sleep with her—and standing here, thinking about it, was pointless.

He strode through his rooms, yanked open the door and headed for the stairs.

A brandy. Two brandies. Then he'd stop this nonsense, go back to his rooms, fall into bed—

What was that? A faint sound. The wind?

The sound came again.

It was the baby.

Rachel had said something about teething. Babies cried when they teethed; he'd heard that or read it somewhere.

Dammit, that was all he needed. A crying child...

The sound stopped.

Karim waited but it didn't come again. Either the child had gone back to sleep or Rachel was soothing him...

Enough thinking about Rachel tonight.

Moonlight dappled the living room, lost itself high in the shadowy darkness of the fourteen-foot ceilings. He went straight to his study, to the teak shelves and a Steuben decanter of—

Hell.

The child was crying again.

He must have been wrong. Rachel wasn't dealing with the boy, but that was her responsibility.

His was to gain custody, see to it the child was raised properly.

As he had been raised.

By tutors and nannies and governesses, so Rami's son would learn to be responsible and not waste his life on frivolity or anything but meeting his obligations...

The crying was annoying.

"Dammit," Karim growled, and he put down the glass, left the study, went quickly up the stairs and down a long corridor to the suite where Rachel and the boy slept.

The sitting room door was shut. He tapped his knuckles against it.

"Rachel?"

No answer.

Great.

She was fast asleep while he paced the floor.

He tried again. Knocked harder, said her name more loudly. Still nothing.

A muscle in his jaw knotted.

"Dammit," he muttered again, and he opened the door and stepped into the sitting room. She had to be in one of the two bedrooms that opened off it.

The noise had stopped but he knew it would start again. There was only one way to deal with it. He'd find Rachel and tell her to keep the child quiet.

He had a full schedule ahead and needed his rest.

He moved briskly through the sitting room. The first door was ajar. He hesitated, then pushed it open.

No crib. No stacks of baby gear—all the stuff he'd arranged to have delivered. He saw only a bed in the same condition as his own, blankets twisted and pushed aside as if the occupant had had difficulty sleeping.

It was Rachel's room. Rachel's bed.

There was the faint scent of lemon in the air. Rachel smelled of lemon. It suited her, that fresh, sweet-sharp tang. It was clean. Delicate.

Honest.

Who but an honest woman would have looked him in the eye when she admitted she'd hated the man who had been her lover?

Then, how had it happened? How could a woman like her have gone to the bed of a man she didn't love?

Karim cursed under his breath.

He was here to deal with a crying baby. Nothing more, nothing less. That his thoughts were wandering was proof that he had to get some sleep if he was going to be able to function well enough tomorrow—actually, today—and put this mess behind him.

He strode back through the sitting room, went straight to the second door.

It, too, was ajar. He stepped inside.

Yes, this was the boy's room. There was the crib. Boxes of baby stuff. The soft illumination of a lamp—what was that, anyway?

A lamp shaped like a carousel.

The work of his assistant?

He'd have to remember to thank her for her creativity, Karim thought wryly...

And then he saw Rachel.

She was asleep in a big wing chair, the baby in her arms. Her hair was loose, falling like a glossy rain over the shoulders of a high-necked white cotton nightgown long enough to cover her feet, which were tucked up under her.

Karim's throat constricted.

He had seen this woman in glitter. In denim. He had seen her naked. She had been beautiful each time, but this, the way she sat now, so unselfconsciously lovely, so perfect and vulnerable, was almost enough to stop his heart.

Whatever the reason she'd been with Rami it didn't matter.

What did matter was that he wanted her more than he'd ever wanted any other woman.

He drew a long, shuddering breath.

But wanting was not the same as having. And he could not have her.

It would only complicate something that was already far too complicated. He had a responsibility. A duty. To his father, his people, his dead brother's memory.

The boy.

That was what this was all about.

His mother had been focused on herself. So had Rami. But he was not like that. He never would be. He—

"Bababababa."

The baby was awake, looking at him through his brother's long-lashed blue eyes. Karim shook his head and put his finger to his lips.

"Shh."

Wrong comment. The child's mouth trembled. He made a little sound, not quite a cry but very close. Karim shook his head again.

"No," he whispered. "Don't. You must let Rachel sleep."

The child's mouth turned down. His small face darkened. Karim moved fast, lifted him carefully from the curve of Rachel's arm and walked quickly into the sitting room.

Now what?

What did you do with a crying child? For that matter, what did you do with one that was not crying?

The boy blew a noisy bubble. Karim looked at him. What the hell did a bubble mean?

"Bzzzt," the kid said.

Karim cleared his throat. He needed a translator.

Little hands waved. Small feet kicked. The round face screwed up.

"Okay," Karim said quickly. "How about we, ah, we go downstairs for a while?"

Down the stairs they went.

The baby began to make little noises. Not happy ones.

"I don't know what you want," Karim said desperately.

God help him if it was a bottle of formula or, worse still, a diaper change.

The living room was lighter now; dawn was touching the soaring towers of the city. Karim went to one of the big, arched windows.

"Look," he said. "It's going to be a sunny day."

More little noises. Karim had a yacht that sounded like that when it started up. Well, no. Not the yacht. The motorboat that could be launched from it—

"Naaah. Naaah. Naaah."

"Shh," Karim said frantically…

Hell.

The kid was crying. Hard. Genuine tears were rolling down his plump cheeks. Karim looked for something to use to wipe them away. Dammit, how come he hadn't thought to put on a T-shirt?

"Don't cry," he said. Carefully, he swiped a finger along the baby's cheeks. A little hand grabbed his finger, dragged it to the rosebud mouth.

The noise stopped.

The tears stopped.

Teething. The kid was teething on his finger.

Karim smiled. He sat down in the corner of one of the curved living room sofas. Put his feet up on the teak and glass coffee table. Carefully arranged himself so there was a throw pillow behind him.

The kid was chomping away. And—*thank you, God*—this time the sounds he made were obviously ones of satisfaction.

"Good, huh?" Karim said softly.

That won him a bubbly smile. Karim smiled back. The kid was cute, if you liked kids. He didn't. Well, no. That wasn't true. He didn't dislike them.

He'd just never spent any time around one.

The kid smelled good, too. Something soft. Not lemony, like Rachel; this was a smell even a man who knew zero about children would automatically associate with babies.

The baby cooed. Smiled around Karim's finger. Karim grinned. And yawned.

The baby yawned, too.

The curving lashes drooped.

"That's it, kid," Karim said softly. "Time to call it a night. You doze off; I'll take you back to Rachel…"

Ethan's lashes fell against his cheeks and didn't lift again.

Karim's did the same.

A moment later, man and baby were sound asleep.

Karim woke abruptly, the baby still in his arms.

Asleep.

An excellent idea. Karim was desperate to do the same thing. Sleep for another couple of hours, then phone his P.A. and tell her to cancel his appointments for the day.

Why not? The guy from Tokyo, the one from India, both could wait until he'd finished dealing with Rami's affairs and had a clear head.

Rami's affairs, he thought, his mouth thinning. That was certainly what Vegas had been all about—his dead brother's affair with a dancer, a stripper, whatever Rachel Donnelly was.

She was also a mother.

A good mother. Hell, an excellent one, from what he'd seen. Responsible. Caring. Determined.

It was surprising that Rami would have been attracted to such a woman. Party girls with boobs bigger than their brains had always been his type.

Not that Rachel lacked anything in that department.

Her breasts, all of her that he'd seen in that quick encounter in her bathroom, were lush and female…

And how many times had he told himself to stop thinking such things, dammit? Because what Rachel was or was not had nothing to do with him or what he had to do next.

Karim got to his feet, carried the baby back to the guest suite. Rachel was still curled in the big chair, asleep.

She looked incredibly beautiful. And innocent.

Amazing how deceiving looks could be.

Amazing how he hungered for her.

He turned away, carefully lowered the baby into the crib, pulled up the blanket, started from the room...

A muscle knotted in his jaw.

He went back to the crib, leaned into it and lightly stroked the boy's soft fair curls.

"Sleep well, little one," he whispered, and then, before he could succumb to the insane desire to go to Rachel and do the same thing, he strode out of the suite, down the corridor to his own rooms, phoned his P.A.—but not to cancel his appointments.

To make more of them.

He'd neglected business for far too long.

Besides, work would clear his head, he told himself as he made a second call, this one to his lawyer, and a third, to the testing laboratory, and cancelled both meetings.

Then he stripped off his sweatpants, got into the shower and let the water beat down on him,

Those things could wait. A day, two—even three.

Putting them off had nothing to do with Rachel.

Nothing at all.

Down the hall, in the guest suite, Rachel, who had awakened as Karim entered the room, opened her eyes only when she was sure he'd gone.

Nothing made sense.

Not the fact that the stern Sheikh had apparently been caring for Ethan while she slept, or that he'd handled the baby with something that could only be defined as tenderness.

And it certainly didn't make sense that as she'd watched him from under her lashes she'd thought what it would be like if he came to her, touched her with those big, gentle hands...

"Fool," she whispered, and she rose to her feet.

It was time to start the day.

And to start planning her escape.

Except escape wasn't possible. There were always eyes on her.

Karim had a household staff.

Rachel knew that he'd told them something about her.

She had no idea what he'd said, but when she appeared in the kitchen that first morning, Ethan in her arms, a bosomy woman with flour-dusted hands had turned from the stove, a polite smile on her lips.

"Good morning, ma'am. I'm Mrs. Jensen, the Sheikh's cook."

And I'm the Sheikh's prisoner, Rachel wanted to say, but she didn't of course, she simply kept her expression neutral,

Karim was the enemy. So, then, was anyone he employed.

"And this is little Ethan. Oh, His Highness was right! He's a beautiful child."

Rachel was surprised.

"Is that what he said?"

"Oh, yes, ma'am. He told us the baby was—"

"Us?"

"Ah." Mrs. Jensen wiped her hands on her apron and pressed a button on the wall phone. "Sorry, ma'am. Prince Karim asked me to be sure and introduce you to the others."

"What others?"

"Why, the rest of the household staff. There's me. And the housekeeper, Mrs. Lopez. The prince's driver—well, you met him at the airport last night. And we've an addition. My granddaughter Roberta. She'll be here within the hour. To help with the baby," the cook added, when she saw the puzzled look on Rachel's face.

"I don't need any help with my baby," Rachel said quickly, drawing Ethan closer.

"You'll like Roberta, ma'am. She's a professional nanny and she adores babies."

"I'm perfectly capable of taking care of Ethan myself."

"Of course you are, Ms. Donnelly. But His Highness asked if my Roberta was available—just, you know, just to help you."

"To keep an eye on me, you mean," Rachel said coldly.

"No, ma'am. Certainly not. To help you, is all." The cook's tone was indignant. "He knows my Roberta's an excellent nanny."

Rachel's voice turned frigid. "Oh, yes," she said, the words heavy with sarcasm. "He'd surely know that."

Mrs. Jensen eyed her with distaste.

"His Highness put Roberta through school, Ms. Donnelly. She'd floundered a bit and he paid for her to have a tutor, and then for her college tuition, until she decided she wanted to work with little ones, so he sent her to a school for nannies."

"Because?"

"I don't understand your question, ma'am."

"Why would he do all that?"

"Because that's how he is," the cook said, her voice almost as chilly as Rachel's. "He honors what he sees as his responsibilities."

"He meddles in people's lives, you mean."

The cook's expression hardened.

"You won't find anyone here who would agree with that, ma'am," she said stiffly.

Fortunately for both Rachel and the cook, the others had chosen that moment to enter the kitchen.

Rachel had been prepared to dislike the entire staff.

She couldn't. How could she dislike people who adored Ethan?

After a couple of days Ethan, the sweet little traitor, adored them right back.

Roberta, in particular.

It was hard to resent her. She didn't interfere at all, and simply gave Rachel a hand when permitted. Finally, Rachel decided it was foolish to take her anger out on a girl only a few years her junior who was a wonder with babies.

Her relationship with the others remained cool.

Surely it was because of whatever Karim had told them about her...

But it wasn't.

One morning, coming down the stairs, she heard Mrs. Lopez and Mrs. Jensen talking in low voices.

"The Prince said she was a nice young woman," Mrs. Jensen was saying, "and that she's had some difficulty lately, but honestly, Miriam, I hate to say it, but I don't think she's nice at all."

"Well," Mrs. Lopez said, "she's wonderful with her baby— anyone can see that. But it's impossible to get a smile from her, isn't it? If I didn't know better, Amelia, I'd think she dislikes us—but why would she, when she hardly know us?"

Damn! Damn! Double damn!

Rachel eased back up the stairs.

Was it possible she'd been wrong about Karim's staff?

Little by little, her dealings with them changed. She smiled; so did they. She said nice things; so did they. She had to admit it made life more pleasant.

As for Karim... She never saw him. What had happened to the meetings with his lawyers? Lab tests?

Rachel didn't ask. Why rush the things she dreaded? Apparently His Sheikhiness was too busy with work to deal with anything else.

She wasn't really surprised. Ethan's welfare would always take second place.

Karim left for his office early in the morning. Not by car. When she asked the reason, strictly as a matter of curiosity—because why would a prince with a Mercedes and a man to drive it leave both behind—John, his driver, said that His Highness generally took the subway.

"Or he walks," he added, and Rachel could almost hear the *tsk-tsk* in the words. "His Highness says it's the best way to beat the traffic."

Big deal, she thought. The mighty Sheikh joins the commoners.

He could travel by broomstick, for all she cared.

And he didn't return until late at night. Very late, never in time for dinner. Their paths never crossed. Fine with her. Excellent, in fact...

And then, one morning, after another night spent walking the floor with Ethan, Rachel finally put him down for a nap. She was too tired to sleep, so went quietly downstairs for coffee.

It was very early. No one would be up and about yet. It meant, she thought, yawning as she stepped into the silent kitchen, that she could show up just as she was, in a long flannel nightgown, her hair loose and her feet bare, put up a pot of coffee and—

The kitchen lights came on.

Rachel gasped, whirled toward the door—

And saw Karim.

He was wearing gray sweatpants, a gray T-shirt with the sleeves cut off, and sneakers that had clearly seen better days. His face and muscled arms glistened with sweat; his hair was in his eyes; his jaw was dark with early-morning stubble...

He was absolutely beautiful.

"I'm sorry—"

"I'm sorry—"

They spoke at the same time. Flustered, Rachel started again.

"I didn't think—"

"I had no idea—"

Their words collided.

Karim grinned, took the towel looped around his neck and dried his face and arms.

Rachel bit her lip, then offered a hesitant smile.

"You first," he said.

She swallowed hard.

"I was going to say that I didn't think I'd be disturbing anyone if—"

"You're not. Disturbing anyone. Disturbing me, I mean," he said. "I just finished working out and I thought—"

"Working out?" she repeated foolishly, because she couldn't seem to think straight. Well, who would? She hadn't expected to see him...

To see him looking so male, so gorgeous, in such a non-princely outfit.

The thought made her laugh. She tried to swallow the laugh, but she wasn't quick enough.

"What?" he said, with a little smile.

"Nothing. It's just—I don't know. I never imagined..."

"What?" he said again, his smile broadening as he looked at her. God, she was easy on the eyes. No make-up. Her hair a golden cloud. Her body hidden beneath the old-fashioned nightgown, just the sweet hint of breasts and hips...

"I, uh, I never thought of you working out."

He grinned. Slapped his incredibly flat belly.

"Have to. Otherwise I'd weigh five hundred pounds."

Rachel laughed. "Somehow, I doubt that."

He moved past her, opened the fridge, took out a container of orange juice.

"Yeah. Well, the truth is, I spend a lot of time behind a desk lately. Not much chance to play sports. And I always did, you know? I still run a little, but when I was in college I played football—"

"Football? Or soccer?"

He looked at her.

"Football. American-style." He smiled. "So, you know they call soccer football everywhere but here in the States, huh?"

She nodded. "When Ethan had colic I used to take him for long drives to soothe him. He loved the motion of the car. Then I'd head home, but I learned, fast that he might wake up if I put him straight into his crib so I'd plop down on the sofa, turn on the TV, and if it was the middle of the night—" she smiled "—which, of course, it almost always was—well, at two and three in the morning there's nothing much on except soccer re-runs—"

"Goooal!" Karim said solemnly.

Rachel laughed. "Right. Oh, and infomercials."

"Infomercials?"

"Yes. You know—men shouting as they try to sell you things you never heard of and never dreamed you needed."

Karim took two glasses from a cabinet, filled them with juice and handed one to Rachel.

"Oh," she said quickly, "no. No, thanks. I, ah, I should get out of your way—"

"You're not in my way. Besides," he said, his expression dead-pan, "if you order this glass of OJ right now, we'll include a cup of coffee at no extra charge. You'll just pay separate shipping and handling."

She burst out laughing. It was as perfect an infomercial as any she'd ever seen.

Karim smiled. "Seriously, I make one heck of a cup of coffee. No shipping or handling charge at all. Okay?"

Not okay, her head told her...

"Okay," she said, because, after all, what harm could there be in something so simple?

He made coffee.

She made toast.

He took his with strawberry jam. She took hers with cream cheese.

"Jam's better," he said.

She shook her head. "Too sweet first thing in the morning."

"I like sweet tastes first thing in the morning," he said, and though he hadn't meant it as a *double entendre* she flushed, and he thought, just for a second, about leaning across the counter and kissing her...

But he didn't.

Somehow this moment, this brief *détente*, was important.

So he cleared his throat, said the weather was unseasonably cool, and then they talked about this and that, the traffic, the newest plans for Central Park...

And then they fell silent.

What if he kisses me? Rachel thought.

I want to kiss her, Karim thought.

Her heartbeat quickened. So did his.

Their eyes met.

"Well..." he said.

"Well..." she said.

They got to their feet.

And moved in opposite directions.

"Got to get moving," he said briskly.

Rachel nodded. "Me, too," she said, just as briskly.

He told himself he was glad he hadn't touched her.

She told herself the same thing.

But those easy moments in the quiet early-morning hours were all either of them thought of that entire day.

The early-morning meeting didn't happen again.

Rachel made sure of that. She didn't leave her room until she was certain Karim was gone.

Yes, she'd discovered her captor had a human side.

So what?

Days passed, and though he didn't mention DNA tests or legal appointments eventually he would.

What would she do then?

Clearly she'd been wrong, thinking she'd be able to take Ethan and fade into the crowd.

She decided she had to confront him.

At the end of a long day—Ethan's first tooth had come in, and he was cutting another—Rachel showered, put on a nightgown, tucked the baby into his crib and settled into the wing chair, pen and notepad in hand.

Time to get organized, she told herself, and began writing.

Contact Legal Aid. Or look up names of attorneys?

Qualifications? General law? Family law?

How to know if a lawyer is a good one?

Would a lawyer work on a payment plan?

Rachel yawned. She was exhausted. A nap. A brief one. And then—and then—

The pad and pen fell to the floor and she dropped into sleep.

CHAPTER NINE

HOURS later, Karim stepped from his private elevator.

The penthouse was silent; lamps glowed discreetly, just enough to chase away the gloom.

Rachel was always in her rooms by now.

And they hadn't run into each other in the morning again.

They couldn't; he'd taken to skipping his workouts. He left even earlier than before.

It was safer that way.

Otherwise, he thought grimly as he loosened his tie and went quietly up the stairs, otherwise he'd—

What?

Take Rachel in his arms? No way. That could only lead to disaster. He was going to take custody of the child. The last thing he needed was to sleep with that child's mother.

Right.

Then, why hadn't he started the ball rolling? Why had he not yet called his lawyer or the DNA lab?

A better question was, why did he walk quietly down the corridor each night, pause outside Rachel's always-closed door, feel his pulse quicken as he imagined himself opening that door, going to her, waking her by taking her in his arms…?

Dammit.

He'd been over this ground before. Hadn't he just thought

the same thing again? The complications if he did such a crazy thing? Even the nasty possibility that her responses to him had been deliberate because she figured she could divert him from his plan?

His body tightened.

Or maybe, like him, she needed to get this impossible hunger out of her system.

Maybe this was the night to do it. Maybe—

What was that?

A sound. A whimper.

It was the baby.

Karim hesitated. He thought of the last time he'd heard the child crying, how he'd found him awake and Rachel asleep...

He stepped forward and opened the door.

It was the same. The dark sitting room. The soft light glowing through the partly open door of the nursery. And Rachel, asleep in the big wing chair, her hair loose and shining against the ivory fabric of one of those old-fashioned nightgowns he'd never known any other woman to wear.

His mistresses wore silk. Or lace. Sexy stuff, meant to turn up the heat...

And never getting it half as high as Rachel did in throat-to-toe cotton.

He wanted to kneel beside her, take her in his arms, draw her down to the floor with him. Kiss her, taste her, make her moan with hunger.

The baby. Concentrate on the baby.

Ethan was in the crib, wide awake, kicking those little arms and legs like a marathon runner and smiling from ear to ear.

Karim smiled back.

"Hey, pal," he whispered.

He moved forward. Stepped on something. A pen and, under it, a notebook. He picked it up, glanced at the page.

Rachel had scrawled a "To Do" list. None of his business what it was...

Except he could see it was about keeping Ethan.

He felt a quick tug of guilt. Which was ridiculous.

He had no reason to feel guilty. The baby was a prince's son. He owed it to his brother's memory, his king and his people, to see to it he was raised as a prince.

"Gaa gaa?"

Karim put the pad and pen on a table, scooped the baby into his arms and tiptoed from the room.

It was close to dawn when something drew Rachel from sleep.

A noise. A stir of sound somewhere in the vast apartment.

"Mmm," she murmured, stretching her arms high over her head.

Falling asleep in this big chair had become something of a habit. It was surprisingly comfortable; she awoke feeling rested and—

"Ethan?"

The crib was empty.

Rachel shot to her feet.

Had he awakened and started to cry and she'd slept through it?

She told herself to calm down.

Ethan was fine. He was somewhere in the apartment and he was fine. But when she found the person who'd taken him instead of waking her—

Barefoot, she made her way down the silent corridor, down the stairs, through the dark rooms...

And ended her search by following the pale flow of light into the big living room, where she found her little boy and her captor.

They were fast asleep.

Rachel's throat constricted.

The room reflected the life and wealth of its owner. White walls. White furniture highlighted by touches of deepest black. It was a sophisticated setting for a sophisticated man…

A man who lay sprawled on one of the long white sofas, shoes, suit coat and tie tossed aside, with Ethan lying spread-eagled against his chest—Ethan so small and sweet in the powerful arms of the powerful man who, except for that first night, behaved as if he didn't exist.

The baby sighed into the tiny damp spot his sore gums had left on what was surely a hand-made white shirt.

Karim drew him closer and, in his sleep, stroked a big hand down Ethan's back.

The baby snuggled in.

Something hot and dangerous flooded Rachel's heart.

No. No, she was not going to let this scene affect her. She knew better, knew what men were, knew what this man was…

Knew that he could be hard as well as tender, not just when he held a baby but when he held her.

She must have made a sound, perhaps a sigh like the baby's, because Karim's dark, thick lashes fluttered, then rose.

His eyes, still blurry with sleep, met hers.

"Ethan was crying." His voice was late-night hoarse. "You were sleeping. I didn't want him to wake you." He paused. Why was she looking at him as if she'd never seen him before? Karim cleared his throat. "So I brought him down here with me."

He fell silent. His heart was racing.

How could she be so beautiful? Such an insignificant word to describe her but it was the only one he had.

She was beautiful.

Her soft, rosy mouth. Her sleep-tousled hair.

And all the rest.

Her breasts, pressing against the thin cotton of her gown. Her long legs, outlined by the soft fabric.

Only the weight of the child against his chest kept him sane, enabled him to raise his eyes to Rachel's without embarrassing them both.

"I'll…" He cleared his throat. "I'll take him upstairs."

"Thank you. For taking care of him."

Karim smiled. "He's a nice little boy."

"Yes. Yes, he is." She swallowed dryly. "I'll take him up."

"That's liable to wake him. Let me."

She nodded. Karim got to his feet and she fell in behind him, followed him up the stairs to the nursery.

She watched him bend over the crib, carefully place the sleeping baby in it. There was a light blanket at the foot; he drew it up, tucked it around the child, touched his pale curls lightly with his hand as he had done that first time.

"Sleep well," he whispered.

Rachel felt a tightness in her chest.

How many times had she held the baby and thought, *If only you were truly mine*…?

Impossible, of course.

Karim's brother and her sister had created this little boy.

But what if fate had written a different story? What if Ethan were not Rami's and Suki's but hers and—and—

She spun away, went into the sitting room and out to the hall.

Karim came after her. "Rachel?"

She was trembling. God, she was—

"Rachel," he said again, "what is it?"

Walk away, she told herself. *Don't be a fool…don't, don't, don't*—

His hand fell on her shoulder. She could feel his hard body behind hers, could feel the heat emanating from him.

He said her name again, his voice low and rough, and she turned and faced him.

What she saw in his eyes told her that tonight, at least, anything was possible.

"Karim," she whispered, and when he reached for her she went straight into his arms.

He told himself there were endless reasons to let go of her. To step back from this while he still could.

He had always done the right thing, the logical thing, the dutiful thing...

Karim groaned, and gathered her close.

This, only this, was the right thing. This was where Rachel belonged.

"Karim."

His name was a sigh on her lips. He looked down into her face, her lovely face, and knew she was feeling the same emotions. Desire. Confusion. The realization that what they were doing could be dangerous, that there would be no going back...

"We can't," she said in a thready whisper, and he said she was right, they couldn't...

She moaned. Rose on her toes. Pressed against him.

He bent to her and captured her mouth.

She tasted of the night, of honey, of herself. She tasted like cream and vanilla, and he shuddered, took the kiss deep, deeper still.

"You are so beautiful," he whispered, and she trembled and wrapped her arms around his neck, and he knew they were both lost.

He slid his hands down her back, cupped her bottom, lifted her into him.

Another groan came from his throat.

He could feel all of her against him now. Her breasts. Her belly. Her hips.

Her body was hot. So was her mouth as he drank from it.

Half the buttons of his shirt were undone and she slid her hands inside, stroked them over his naked shoulders, and he shuddered under that feather-soft, tantalizing touch.

He drew her closer, holding her as if his arms were bands of steel, but it wasn't enough, it couldn't be enough—not when the need to make her his pounded through him with every beat of his heart.

He wanted to sweep her into his arms. Carry her to his bed.

But first—first just a taste of her skin. Here, behind her ear. Here, in the tender hollow of her throat. Here, at the delicate juncture of neck and shoulder.

She cried out.

The sound raced through him like a river of flame.

"Do you want this?' he whispered. "Tell me, *habibi*. Tell me what you want."

She cupped his face, dragged it down to hers and kissed him.

"This," she whispered. "You. But we can't. We can't—"

His kiss was hot and hard. Her knees buckled; he swung her up into his arms, his mouth never leaving hers, and carried her to his bedroom.

Moonlight poured in through the windows, spilling over them in a pool of ivory iridescence. He put her on her feet beside his bed and his eyes locked on her face.

"Tell me to stop," he said thickly, "and I will. But tell me now, before it's too late. Do you understand, Rachel? Once I start to touch you—once I start there's no going back."

The room filled with silence broken only by the rasp of his breath. Then, slowly, she brought her hands to the top button of her nightgown.

Karim's hand closed on hers.

"Let me undress you."

He heard the catch of her breath. Her hands fell to her sides. He reached for the first of what were surely a thousand buttons, none made for male fingers as big and suddenly clumsy as his, but he wanted to be the one who bared her to his eyes.

One button gave way.

Two.

Three.

And finally he could see—ah, God—he could see the slope of her breasts.

"Karim," she whispered.

He tore his gaze from her breasts, fixed his eyes on her face. Saw her parted lips, the flush of desire that streaked her cheeks, the darkness of her pupils.

His throat constricted. He leaned forward, kissed her mouth.

And undid the next button.

And the one after that.

Undid them, button by button, until there were none left.

Slowly, the gown parted.

And he saw her.

Saw all of her. Naked and incredibly lovely.

Her breasts were small and round, and he knew instantly that they were meant to fit perfectly in his cupped palms.

Her nipples were elegant buds, their color the dusty pink of the early-summer roses that grew wild in the valleys of the Great Wilderness Mountains.

Her hips were lushly feminine curves, the perfect framework for the soft curls at the junction of her thighs.

God, he needed to touch her.

Cup her breasts with his hands. Brush his fingers over her erect nipples. Put his mouth to the heart of her, let her feel the heat of his tongue between her thighs.

He looked up. Watched her face. Reached out slowly,

brushed his fingers over her nipples. She gasped, and he
bent his head, kissed her mouth, her throat, her breasts...

Drew one rosy bud between his lips.

She sobbed his name, shuddered. Her head fell back and
she cried out with pleasure.

It almost undid him.

He drew her down with him onto the bed. Go slow, he told
himself. Go slow...

Her body was hot against his.

Her mouth was soft.

And his erection was so hard it was almost painful.

"Rachel," he said unsteadily, and she wound her arms
around his neck, and somehow, somehow, her nightgown
was ruched around her hips and somehow, somehow, his
hand was between her thighs and she was wet and hot and
slick, and he found that sweet nub that was the essence of
her, and when he did she arched against his hand and gave
a cry that made him rear back, tear off his clothes and pull
open the drawer of the nightstand.

He found a condom. Fumbled with it. And then—

Then he was inside her.

A groan tore from his throat.

Rachel was tight around him, so tight he was afraid he'd
hurt her, and he went still, his body trembling with the effort, holding back, letting her stretch to accommodate him.
But she wouldn't let that happen. She was sobbing, moving
against him, moving, moving, moving...

She said his name. He could feel her trembling; she was
on that razor-thin edge of eternity with him.

Could a man's entire life have been meant to bring him
to this one moment?

He thrust forward, harder, deeper, faster. She whispered
his name again and then she screamed in ecstasy.

And Karim let go of everything—the pain of the last

weeks, the rigidity of his life—and flew with her along the moonlit path into the heart of the night sky.

He collapsed over her, his body slick with sweat.

His face was buried in the curve of her shoulder, her hair was a silken tangle and he loved the feel of it against his lips. His heart was pounding; so was hers. He could feel it beating hard against his.

He knew he was too heavy for her but he didn't want to move—not if it meant giving up this moment. Rachel's skin against his skin, her arms around him, her legs wrapped around his hips…

She gave a little sigh.

He sighed, too, rolled to his side and drew her into his arms.

"Are you all right?" he said softly.

She nodded. "I'm fine."

"Very fine?" he said, and smiled. He used one hand to tilt her face to his. "Incredibly fine?" he whispered, and kissed her.

Her lips were soft. They clung to his but only for a heartbeat. Then she drew back.

"I—I have to get up," she whispered.

"Not yet," he said in a sexy, rough voice as he stroked a lock of hair from her temple and tucked it behind her ear. "Stay with me a little longer."

"No. Really. I have to—I have to get up."

A simple request, Karim told himself. She wanted to use the bathroom. A simple, normal request.

But her voice was strained and her eyes darted away from his.

"Rachel?"

She didn't answer.

"Rachel. Sweetheart—"

"Let me up!"

For a horrible few seconds she was afraid he was going to keep his arms where they were, one around her shoulders, the other draped over her waist, but finally he let her go.

Now the trick was to sit up and not let him see her, because she was naked and, yes, he'd already seen her, he'd more than seen her...

Somehow, she managed to struggle upright and drag the edges of her nightgown together. Then she got to her feet, her back to him.

"Where are you going?"

He didn't sound sexy anymore. No matter. She would sound brisk and bright.

"To the bathroom."

Karim sat up. "The bathroom's behind you."

"The bathroom in the guest suite."

"What's going on, Rachel? You have regrets?"

"Honestly, Karim, I'd think you would know that there's nothing less appealing than a—a post-sex analysis. So if you don't mind—"

She turned away from him and started for the door, her posture stiff and unyielding. He grabbed his discarded trousers, pulled them on, got to the door before she did, stood with his back to it, arms folded over his chest, legs slightly apart, face without expression.

"Please," she said. "Get out of my way."

"Not until you talk to me."

"I told you, I have to go to the—"

"You're running away."

Her head came up. "The hell I am," she snapped.

So much for brisk and bright.

"A minute ago you were in my arms. And now—"

"And now it's over. You got what you wanted."

She cried out as his hands closed on her shoulders.

"Don't," he growled.

"Don't what? Tell the truth? Dammit, let go of me!"

"We made love. Don't try to turn it into something ugly."

"We went to bed." Her eyes flashed. "Don't try to turn it into something pretty."

His mouth twisted.

"Next thing I know," he said, very softly, "you're going to claim I forced you."

"No." Her chin lifted; color striped her cheekbones. "I'm not. There are already too many—too many lies between us!"

"For instance."

"For instance— For instance—"

Rachel fell silent. It was one lie, one huge lie, that lay between them, but she couldn't tell him that. If he knew the truth he'd have all the ammunition he needed to take Ethan from her.

"I'm waiting," he said coldly. "Exactly what lies are you talking about?"

She looked up. Moistened her lips with the tip of her tongue.

"There's really no point to this," she said wearily. "We did—what we did. And now—"

"And now you want to forget it ever happened."

Yes, she wanted to say, but that would be an even greater lie. She knew she'd never forget being with Karim. Never.

"I just—I just want to move on."

Karim's eyes darkened.

"Move on?"

"Yes. You know, this was—it was nice, but—"

He cupped her face, cut off her words with a kiss. She fought it, but only for a second. Then she gave a soft little cry, put her arms around his neck and gave herself up to him.

When he finally took his mouth from hers she was shaking.

"We can't," she whispered.

"We already did," he said. "And I wouldn't change it for all the riches of the world, sweetheart." He paused. "And neither would you." His voice softened. "Tell me that isn't true and I'll let you walk away."

Here was her chance.

He was a man of honor. She knew that already. If she said, *What just happened means nothing to me,* he would let her turn her back on this—whatever "this" was.

But she couldn't say those words—couldn't turn what had been so beautiful into something ugly.

"Karim—"

"I like the way you say my name."

"You don't know anything about me."

He smiled. "I know that you're hell on my ego. And that's a lot, coming from a man who's— What was it you called me? Arrogant. Self-centered. A despot." Another smile. "Did I leave anything out?"

"We'd just met. And—and I know you won't believe me, but I don't do—I don't do—"

"Do what?" he said solemnly.

Color swept into her face.

"I'm not the woman you think I am." That, at least, was true. "And I don't go to bed with—with strange men."

"I'm strange, huh?"

"No! I didn't mean—"

"That's okay," he said, even more solemnly. "Don't hold back. Just say what you think."

There was laughter in his eyes. She could feel a smile trying to form on her lips but there was nothing to smile about—certainly not to laugh about.

"You're impossible," she said. "I'm trying to be serious."

"So am I." He bent to her, kissed her with a tenderness

she knew she didn't deserve. "You think this is wrong be-cause—because of Rami."

The weight of her deception made it hard to breathe. She nodded; how could she trust herself to speak?

"Because," he said gruffly, "you slept with him."

"Karim, please. I don't want to—"

"No. Neither do I. Hell, Rami's the last thing I want to talk about right now."

"You think—you think I cared for him. But—"

"No. I don't. You said you hated him, remember?" His dark eyes narrowed. "But we can't pretend you and he…" He took a long, harsh breath. "You slept with him. You bore his child."

A sob burst from Rachel's throat. She spun away, but Karim caught her, turned her toward him.

"You think I need to hear the reasons?" His eyes met hers. "I don't. What happened is in the past. Now, today, tomor-row…that's what matters." His voice turned husky. "Besides, if there is one thing I know with all my heart it is that you may have slept with Rami—but you and I just made love."

Tears rose in her eyes.

"We made love," he said fiercely. "You know it. I know it. Why won't you admit it?"

"Because—because—"

She gave a muffled sob. Karim cursed and gathered her in his arms. She buried her face against him and her hot tears fell on his bare chest.

"I don't give a damn about anything that happened be-fore we met," he said, his voice raw. "This. Us. That's all that matters."

"There is no 'us.' There can't be. I told you—you don't know anything about me…"

He bent his head, took her mouth in a hard, quick kiss.

"I know everything I need to know," he said roughly.

"You're brave. And strong. You face life with dignity and courage."

Guilt was sharp as the thrust of a knife into her heart.

Tell him, a voice within her whispered. *You must tell him. You have to...you have to—*

"I was wrong to say I'd take your son from you."

Oh, God! "Karim," she said quickly. "Karim. About— about the baby—"

"No. You don't have to say anything, *habibi.* You are a good mother. A wonderful mother. We'll find a way around this." His expression softened; he smiled and ran his thumb gently over her mouth. "And you're beautiful," he said softly. "Not just your face and your body. Inside, where it counts, you're the most beautiful woman in the world. So you see? I know all I need to know about you." His smile broadened. "Except, perhaps, what you would like for a midnight snack."

Rachel looked into the eyes of this man who had turned out to be nothing like his brother, nothing like any man she'd ever known.

Despite herself, her lips curved in an answering smile.

"You're changing the subject, Your Highness."

"Aha. Progress." His tone was solemn, but his eyes were filled with laughter. "That's the first time you've used those words without making me cringe."

Her smile broadened. "Don't let it go to your head, but you can be a very nice man."

He grinned.

"For an arrogant, self-centered despot, you mean?"

Rachel laid her hand against Karim's jaw. It was rough with end-of-day stubble. It made him look dangerous and incredibly sexy.

"Maybe I was wrong about that."

"You were right, *habibi.* I am all those things—but not when I am with you." He caught her hand, pressed a kiss into her palm. "On second thought…" His voice turned as rough as that stubble. "On second thought…" His teeth sank lightly into the flesh at the base of her thumb. "Are you hungry, too, sweetheart?"

Rachel looked up into her lover's dark eyes and answered the question she saw there.

"Yes," she whispered. "I'm hungry for you."

Karim groaned, brought her hard against him and kissed her.

The world, and the web of lies she had created, spun away.

CHAPTER TEN

Now they could make love more slowly.

There was time to learn each other's most intimate secrets, to explore with slow hands and deep kisses, to speak in a lovers' language of soft whispers and softer sighs.

"I love the taste of you," Karim said as he lay back with Rachel in his arms.

God, he did.

Her skin was silk against his lips, her nipples honey-tipped buds. Her scent was intoxicating, pure and female. Everything about her heightened his desire: the way she moaned when he caressed her, the curve of her mouth against his, the blurring of her eyes when he entered her.

He enjoyed sex, and there was no sense in not admitting he was an accomplished lover. Still, a part of him always remained a little removed during the act, and if he'd given it any thought he'd have said that was a good thing; it meant he could hold on to his self-control until the last possible second.

Not with Rachel.

He couldn't tell where her pleasure began and his ended.

It was an incredible sensation.

And when she grew bolder and began to explore him—touching the tip of her tongue to his salty skin, lightly bit-

ing his lip, running her hands over his muscled shoulders
and arms—

He almost went crazy.

He wanted to tumble her on her back, drive into her until
the earth trembled.

Somehow he forced himself to keep from doing it—

Like now, when her hand moved lower.

And stilled.

Karim whispered her name. She looked up. Her eyes
were pools of hot darkness; *I could drown in those eyes,* he
thought, *and die happy.*

"Touch me," he said thickly.

Rachel had never wanted to touch a man so intimately,
never really looked at a man's hard, erect flesh.

Now she wanted to do both.

It took less courage to look. She did, and caught her breath.

This part of her lover that gave her such pleasure was
beautiful, a symbol not only of his virility but of his desire
for her.

"Rachel."

Karim's voice was low. Strained. Gently, he clasped her
wrist and brought her hand closer.

And waited, barely breathing.

Slowly, slowly enough so he could feel the sweat gathering on his forehead, he watched her reach out.

Her fingers brushed his taut flesh.

He groaned.

She jerked back.

"I don't—I don't want to hurt you…"

Did a man laugh or cry at such a moment?

"You won't hurt me," he said, his voice gruff. He made a
sound he hoped was a laugh. "You may kill me, *habibi,* but
you won't hurt me."

Rachel slicked the tip of her tongue over her bottom lip.

Karim bit back another groan—and then she closed her hand around him.

He shuddered.

"Yes," he whispered, "yes, sweetheart. That's it. Touch me like that. Like that…"

His hand closed over hers; he taught her how to make that soft groan rise in his throat again, but now she understood that it wasn't a sound of pain.

It was pleasure.

Pleasure only she could bring him.

She saw it in his face, the way his golden skin seemed to tighten over the bones, the way his nostrils flared…

Until he caught her wrist again and stopped her.

"Wait," he said thickly.

He took a long, deep breath. Expelled it. Another breath. Then he leaned toward her.

"My turn," he whispered.

He eased her onto her back. Knelt between her thighs. Kissed her mouth. Her throat. Her breasts.

It was she who groaned this time, and moved restlessly under his caresses.

"I love watching you," he said softly. "The rise of color in your face. The way your lashes veil your eyes. I love seeing what happens to you when I touch you. When I kiss you. When I do this…"

She gasped as he parted her with his fingers. Stroked her, then bent to her, licked her, sucked on her. She came on a dizzying wave of release.

But there was more.

First, another condom.

Then he brought the head of his erect penis against her silken folds.

"Look," he said. "Watch me enter you, *habibi*."

His words made her tremble with anticipation.

She raised her head, looked at the place where their bodies met in the most intimate of kisses.

"Watch," he said again, his voice rough as gravel.

She watched. Cried out at the sweet, sweet torture of seeing him penetrate her, feeling him claim her.

"Rachel…"

He thrust hard, thrust deep, and she gave a long, wild sob of joy, fingers clenched around his biceps, her legs wrapped high around his hips.

Karim's body glistened with sweat. His heart was racing. He wanted to follow her into oblivion…

Teeth gritted, he fought against it.

And took her to the brink again.

It was too much.

She could feel herself starting to come apart.

"Please," she sobbed, "please, Karim, please…"

He drove deep one final time.

And as she screamed he let go, spent himself within her silken walls, then collapsed in her arms.

The moments slipped by.

Then Karim lifted his head, brushed his lips gently over hers and rolled to his side with Rachel safe in his arms.

She gave him a slow, sweet kiss. And she smiled.

It was the kind of smile a man dreamt of seeing on the face of the woman he'd just made love with, and he smiled back.

Hell, he grinned.

"I take it," he said, trying to sound solemn but not succeeding, "that smile signifies satisfaction."

"In triplicate," she said softly.

He gave a soft, delighted laugh. She smiled again.

"No pretensions at modesty, Your Highness?"

"None whatsoever," he said, "because you're the reason this was so wonderful, *habibi*. So incredibly perfect."

He brought his mouth to hers for a tender, lingering kiss, and when she sighed against his lips he felt his heart swell.

"Perfect," he murmured.

Rachel closed her eyes, put her head on his shoulder, her hand over his heart.

"What does that mean? *Habibi*?"

"It means sweetheart," he said, pressing a kiss into her hair.

"In Arabic, yes?"

He nodded. "Yes. It was my first language."

She raised her head, moved her hand just enough so she could prop her chin on it.

God, she was beautiful!

Her hair was a tangle of soft waves around her face. Their lovemaking had turned her eyes bright and given her skin a pink glow.

He wanted to rise over her and make love to her again.

"Your first language? You mean, before English?"

"Before French. Then I learned English. And Spanish. And German. And... What?"

"Five languages?"

"Six. Well, almost six. I'm still having trouble with Japanese."

She laughed.

"I'm still having trouble with Spanish," she said, "which is pretty sad, considering that I took a year of it in high school. Of course that was a long time back."

"I'll bet it was," Karim said as seriously as possible. "What was it? Twenty years ago? Twenty-five?"

Rachel balled her fist and punched him lightly in the belly.

"Oof! Okay, not twenty-five."

"I was in high school seven years ago, Sir Sheikh," she said, trying to sound indignant.

"Sir Sheikh, huh?" He smiled, brushed a strand of glossy hair back from her cheek. "I'll bet you were an honors student."

A cloud seemed to darken her eyes.

"I wasn't."

"Too busy being the homecoming queen to study?"

She stared at him for what seemed a long time. Then she rolled away, sat up, grabbed the comforter and wrapped it around herself like an oversized cloak.

"Rachel." Karim moved fast, caught her hand before she could get to her feet. "Sweetheart, what did I say?"

"Nothing."

"Don't do this. If I said something that hurt you, tell me."

The tension in her damned near radiated through his hand.

"Remember what I told you? That there are lots of things you don't know about me? Well, here's one of them. I didn't graduate from high school. I finally qualified for an equivalency diploma a couple of years ago and that's how come I'm still struggling with Spanish—because I only began taking it again in night classes at college. So, no, I don't speak six languages, and, no, I don't have a university degree, and, no—"

Karim swung her toward him and stopped the flow of angry, pained words with a kiss.

"I couldn't stay in school," Rachel said in a low voice when he lifted his lips from hers. "I had to take care of my sister and me."

"Your parents?" Karim said, trying to sound calm.

She shook her head. "My father died when Suki and I were little. My mother—my mother liked to have fun. She went away one day and we never saw her again."

"You see?" he said, trying to conceal the rage he felt at a

woman he had never laid eyes on. "We have something in common. My mother left Rami and me, too."

"It's hard—it's hard to know how a mother could—could—"

Karim cursed, pulled her into his lap and kissed her.

"*Habibi,*" he whispered. "*Habibi. Ana behibek—*"

"What does that mean?"

He swallowed hard.

"It means—it means you are very brave, sweetheart. It means I love holding you in my arms."

"I'm not brave at all," she said in a wobbly voice, and Karim tumbled back on the bed with her because the only safe way to show her that she was everything he'd just said was to make love to her again.

There was nothing at all safe in telling her the truth—

That what he'd really said was that he loved her.

They slept locked in each other's arms.

Sunlight woke them.

Karim looked into Rachel's eyes.

"Good morning," he said softly.

Rachel smiled. "Good morning."

"Did you sleep well?"

"Wonderfully well. In fact…" She rose on her elbow and looked past him to the iPod docked on the nightstand. "Oh! It's past seven. Ethan—"

"Ethan is fine."

"But—"

"Really. I checked a little while ago. Roberta has him downstairs. She's feeding him some unidentifiable yellow slop mixed with some equally unidentifiable white slop."

Rachel laughed at her lover's excellent description of strained peaches combined with rice cereal.

"He loves that slop," she said

"Which only proves Ethan's a baby. She says she's going to take him to the park when he's finished eating."

"Then I'd better hurry and get showered and—"

"I'm a man of the desert, *habibi*."

"Meaning...?"

"Meaning," he said, looking very serious, "I understand things you do not."

"Such as?"

"Water is a precious commodity. So saving water is an imperative." His mouth twitched. "Therefore we must make the sacrifice of showering together."

Rachel smiled. "And a lovely sacrifice it would be," she said softly, "but if Roberta's taking Ethan to Central Park..."

"She loves the boy, Rachel."

"I know. She's wonderful with him, and—"

"And she has a very impressive certificate from a very fancy school."

Rachel nodded.

"Yes. And you paid her tuition."

"Mrs. Jensen told you about that?"

"She certainly— Karim! You're blushing!"

"I am not blushing," he said, blushing harder.

"First tutoring. Then college. Then nanny school." She kissed his chin. "You really are a very nice man."

Karim smiled.

"What I am," he said, "is a man in desperate need of food."

"That's it. Change the subject." She sighed. "Ethan will have a fine time with Roberta. And you do need food. We both do."

"I love knowing I've given you an appetite."

It was Rachel's turn to blush. She put her palms against his chest and gave him a gentle shove.

"I'll make us some breakfast."

"And force Mrs. Jensen out of her own kitchen?"

"Oh. I didn't think of—"

"I'd love to have you make breakfast, sweetheart."

"But Mrs. Jensen—"

Karim gathered her to him. "I'll send her to the market."

Rachel batted her lashes.

"Such a wise man, Your Highness!"

"Training," he said loftily. "When a man is destined to be king, he knows how to keep the peace."

Her teasing smile faded.

"For a little while," she whispered, "I almost forgot that."

Yes. So had he. But now there it was. Reality. The commitment to duty. Honor. Responsibility. The very things that had brought this woman into his life.

There was only one problem.

He had never expected to fall in love with her.

But he had. She was everything to him.

How could that be?

She had been Rami's.

No. She had said it herself. No one was anyone's property. Besides, he had told her that the past didn't matter.

And he meant it.

It didn't.

What mattered was that he loved Rachel. She was good and kind and honest; he had never let himself even imagine finding a woman like her to complete him, and that was what she did.

She completed him...

The breath caught in his throat.

Suddenly he saw a path ahead of him—one that would enable him to fulfill his duties, maintain his honor, meet his responsibilities to his father, his country, his dead brother and his brother's child.

In one simple step he could do all those things and keep

the promise he'd made to Rachel about finding a way she could keep Ethan…

Be truthful, Karim.

Those things were all important…but they were not the real reason for what he was about to do.

Duty was important.

But love was everything. Everything—

"Karim?"

He blinked, looked into the face of the woman he loved. She looked worried. For him. And wasn't that amazing? Had he ever thought a woman would care for him, the man, and not for him, the Sheikh?

"Karim. Please, talk to me. What's wrong?"

"Nothing," he said—and then he gave a whoop of laughter, tugged her to her feet, whirled her around the room to music only he could hear and, when she was breathless and laughing with him, brought them to a halt and took her in his arms.

"Remember when I promised you I'd find a solution for our problem?"

Their problem.

Ah, God!

In her joy these last hours Rachel had managed to tuck reality aside. Now it had returned.

"Yes," she said slowly. "I remember. You want Ethan."

He nodded and drew her closer.

"At first he was all I wanted."

"You said—you said you wouldn't take him from me…"

"Sweetheart." Karim cleared his throat. Framed her face with his hands, lifted it to his. "The answer to our problem is to see that it isn't a problem at all."

"But it is. I wish it weren't, but—"

"I love you, *habibi*."

His voice was gruff; his words were the most beautiful

she'd ever heard. Tears stung her eyes. He kissed them away, then kissed her mouth, gently and tenderly.

"Rachel." He took a deep breath. "I've lived my life alone. By choice. I—I don't want to sound like one of those TV shows where people put their emotions on display." He gave a small laugh. "Hell, there've been times I've been told I don't have emotions."

Rachel shook her head. "You're a wonderful man," she said fiercely, "with a heart as big as the world."

"A heart you have awakened, *habibi*." He kissed her again, his mouth soft against hers. "What I said…that I love you…I've never said those words before. Not to anyone." He paused. "And I've never trusted anyone fully. Never—not since I was a little boy." He smiled. "And then—and then I found you."

Tears rose in Rachel's eyes. This was it. She had to tell him the truth, no matter what the cost…

"Rachel." Karim looked deep into her eyes. "Marry me. Become my wife. The mother to the children we will have together as you already are to Ethan, who I've come to love as my own, who I will adopt and give my name."

Rachel began weeping.

"Rachel? Sweetheart, I adore you. I thought—I thought you felt the same—"

She flung her arms around his neck. Lifted herself to him. Kissed his mouth with all the love he had brought to her lonely heart.

"I love you," she whispered, between kisses. "I love you, love you, love you—"

"Marry me," Karim said.

No, a voice inside her whispered. *Rachel, you mustn't…*

"Rachel?"

Rachel threw caution to the wind and said, "Yes."

CHAPTER ELEVEN

Who would have thought that busy, crowded, shark-eat-shark Manhattan could be a paradise for lovers?

Not Karim.

He knew the city the way he knew London and Paris and Istanbul, knew its hotels, its restaurants, its business centers.

And, though he wasn't given to musing about romance, if pressed, he'd have said those cities were probably romantic.

Paris had a unique beauty and charm. Istanbul had a mystery that came of the blended cultures of east and west. London had crooked streets layered in history.

But New York? Frenetic. Impatient. Crowded. Rude. Boisterous.

And yet magnificent.

Those were the words that described his adopted home.

But romantic? No. That was what he would have said, had anyone asked. Had he even thought about such things. Which he didn't, because, after all, what did *he* know of romance? What place did it have in his life?

Not a thing—until ten days ago.

Rachel had changed his life.

He had lived in New York for a decade. And yet he knew he'd never really seen it before.

Central Park was no longer just a place for an early-morning run. It was, instead, a stretch of green as beautiful as the forested slopes that rose above his desert home. The cobbled streets of SoHo and Greenwich Village weren't places to avoid because of the traffic; they were as delightful to stroll as Montmartre.

Hand in hand, they explored the city together. They discovered quite cafés, pretty little parks, places where a man and woman could be alone despite the crowds all around them.

He managed a small miracle, too, when he finally convinced his bride-to-be that there was nothing wrong in letting him take her into half a dozen elegant boutiques and buying her soft, summery dresses, delicate lingerie and pairs of shoes that made her ooh and ahh with delight.

Heels? Yes.

"But no stilettos," she said, with a mock shudder.

That was when he learned she hadn't been a dancer, that she'd been a waitress, that she'd hated the shoes and the spangles and the thong, and her expression had turned so grave that right there, at the crowded intersection of Spring and Mercer, he'd taken her in his arms and kissed her.

In all the ways that mattered, the city was almost as new to Karim as it was to Rachel.

Even the restaurants he took her to were places he'd never seen before…except he had. He'd taken clients to the Four Seasons, to Daniel, to La Grenouille, but they were different places when he went to them with the woman he loved.

The woman he loved, he thought as he and Rachel sat at an intimate table for two in the River Café, the lights of Manhattan reflected in the dark, deep waters of the East River visible through the wall of windows beside them.

Karim's mouth curved in a very private smile.

He loved Rachel. And she loved him. He was still trying to get used to the idea.

There was so much to get his head around—starting with

coming awake each morning with her in his arms and ending with falling asleep that same way each night.

He'd gone to his office only twice. Even he found that unbelievable. He knew his staff damned well did.

He'd had good intentions the first time he'd gone to work, but he'd left before hardly anyone had known he was there. He'd thought about phoning John for his car, thought of flagging a taxi, but the streets had been clogged with vehicles, as always, and the fastest way home was to jog.

Which was what he'd done.

One hell of a sight, he was sure, a guy running up Madison Avenue in a Brioni suit and Gucci loafers, then rushing from the elevator into the foyer of his penthouse.

"Rachel?" he'd shouted. "Rachel?"

"Karim?" she'd said, from the top of the stairs. "What's the matter?"

"Nothing," he'd replied, taking the stairs two at a time. "Everything," he'd added, scooping her into his arms and kissing her. "I missed you," he whispered, and her face had lit with such joy that he'd carried her straight back to bed.

The second time he'd gone to his office he'd stayed just long enough to go through his calendar, assign whatever had to be dealt with to members of his administrative staff, and instruct his P.A. to cancel his appointments and to tell anyone trying to reach him that he was unavailable.

His P.A. had looked at him as if he'd lost his sanity.

"Unavailable, sir?"

"Unavailable," Karim had said firmly.

Because he was. Unavailable. Unreachable. Incommunicado to anyone but Rachel.

Or Ethan.

The baby was, without doubt, the smartest, most adorable kid in the world.

He giggled with delight when Karim introduced him to

the wonders of "I See." Belly-laughed when Karim lifted him high in the air. Adored having Karim blow bubbles against his tummy.

Laughter, and the love that accompanied it, was not something Karim or Rami had experienced much in their childhoods.

Which had turned him into a man with a heart so well disguised it had been all but non-existent, and Rami into a man who'd frittered his life away.

In some small measure, Karim hoped he could make up for the emptiness of Rami's existence by raising his son with all the love possible.

The best part was that it was easy to do.

Who'd have thought that he, the all-powerful Sheikh of Wall Street—a laughable title dumped on him in some foolish internet blog—would change diapers, do feedings, walk the floor with a crying child in his arms, sit in the park with Rachel and a baby carriage and be so content that half the time he suspected he had a goofy grin on his face?

God, he was happy.

Though sometimes he caught a look in Rachel's eyes that worried him.

A darkness.

Maybe he only imagined it.

He had to be imagining it—except there it was again, right now, as she looked out the window of the restaurant into the night: a sudden shift from smiling to something that wasn't quite a smile, as if a thought, a memory, had surfaced and brought her pain.

"Sweetheart?" he said softly. He saw her throat constrict as she swallowed. When she turned to him her smile was a smile again. Karim brought her hand to his lips. "Are you okay?"

"Yes."

"You sure? You looked—I don't know. Sad."

She shook her head, brought their joined hands to her own lips and kissed his knuckles.

"How could I be sad when I'm with you? I was just—I was just thinking how beautiful it is here."

"You're what's beautiful," Karim said.

And Rachel thought, as she had thought just a moment ago, *If only lies could be untold. If only time would stand still.*

Growing up, she'd loathed the slow passage of time.

Of course she knew time moved at only one speed. Sure, she'd bounced from school to school, but she'd read a lot. She'd read everything she could get her hands on.

"Pay half as much attention to how you look as you do to those books," Mama would say, "you'll be a happier girl."

But knowing time could move like molasses dripping from a cold jug had nothing to do with book-learning.

It had to do with…well, with her life.

Mama meeting a new man. Weeks or months taking on a snail's pace while she lavished all her attention on him until the new man became old news. Then Mama would haul their suitcases from under the bed. A day later they'd be on the Greyhound again, heading for a new town.

That was the only time things moved fast. After that…

A new town. New school. New kids. Rachel not fitting in. Suki running wild. And, always, a new man for Mama.

And time would once again grind to a halt, until Mama would get that look on her face, make her usual little speech about being tired of Jim or Bill or Art, or whatever man had just dumped her, and the entire sad pattern would start over.

So, no.

Rachel had never hoped time would stand still. She'd wanted it to rush on by…

Because she'd never been happy.

It had taken her twenty-four years to figure it out. When you were happy, time standing still was exactly what you wanted.

The first time she'd felt that way was the day Suki had handed Ethan to her.

And now there was this.

There was Karim.

She loved him. She adored him. There were moments she could hardly breathe for the joy in her heart.

Sitting here tonight, her lover across from her, his big hand clasping hers, seeing him smile, having him feed her bits of his lobster, hearing his rough whisper of warning about what he was liable to do if she parted her lips and showed him the tip of her tongue one more time...

If he'd grabbed her from her chair and carried her from the restaurant she'd have let him do it.

Over dinner, he'd talked about his childhood. Like the time he'd sneaked into the palace stables, selected his father's favorite stallion, put on the bit, bridle and reins and ridden bareback over the desert until his father's men caught up to him hours later and brought him back.

"My father was furious."

"I'll bet. What if the horse had thrown you?"

"He cared about the horse, *habibi*. He'd paid hundreds of thousands of dollars for it. And I was only seven. Not really big enough to control the animal."

"He wasn't worried about you? Oh, that's terrible!"

"And that's very nice."

"What is?"

"The way that tempting mouth of yours just dropped open, as if it needs me to kiss it." He brought her hand to his lips and bit lightly into it. "Perhaps other parts of you need kissing, too."

"Hush," she whispered. "What if someone hears you?"

But she was smiling, and he could tell by the pink blush on her face that what he'd said had pleased her.

Which was excellent, considering that all he wanted was to please her...

Especially tonight. With dessert.

A very special dessert, he thought, as their waiter approached the table.

"Your Highness. Miss." The waiter grinned. Karim gave him a warning look and the guy quickly cleared his throat. "The chef sends his compliments and says he's prepared a special dessert." He shot Rachel a big smile. "In the lady's honor."

"For me?" she said with delight.

"Yes, ma'am. If you're ready, sir...?"

Karim nodded. He was ready. Nervous, but ready.

After almost two weeks together, he still couldn't believe his luck.

That he'd gone to Las Vegas to try to put right the problems his brother had left and had, instead, met this wonderful woman.

What a fool you were, Rami, he thought.

And yet he had Rami to thank for this miracle. Rachel. Her little boy.

He'd have liked to be able to tell him that.

They had been close, once upon a time. Now, in some strange way, he felt close to Rami again.

The only thing that troubled him was trying to accept that Rachel had—had been with Rami.

It wasn't about sex.

Okay.

Maybe it was, a little.

But he wasn't a male chauvinist. He came from a culture where women had, until relatively recently, been denied the rights to which men were born, but he'd never considered virginity something he'd demand in a wife.

The problem went beyond that.

He could not imagine Rami and Rachel having a conversation together, much less sleeping together. Rami had been all about the way a woman looked. Rachel was beautiful, but she was much more than that.

She was bright. Articulate. Opinionated.

Definitely opinionated.

He'd been reading a political blog on his laptop this morning; she'd been reading the same blog on his iPad. He hadn't known she was reading it and he'd mumbled something about it to himself. She'd mumbled back, and the next thing he knew she'd been debating with him for all she was worth.

Rami wouldn't have given a damn.

He loved it.

Loved her—which brought him back to the beginning. How could there have been anything between two such different people?

He wanted to ask.

But he didn't.

For one thing, Rachel had made it clear she didn't want to talk about the time she'd spent with Rami.

For another, he wasn't sure he'd be comfortable with the answers.

As he'd told her at the beginning, it was best to leave the past in the past and concentrate on today. On right now— because the waiter was coming with dessert.

A fanciful, miniature chocolate Brooklyn Bridge for him...

A scoop of vanilla ice cream for her.

The waiter put the dishes in front of them, shot a conspiratorial grin at Karim, said, "Enjoy!" and almost skipped away.

Karim watched Rachel look from his little bridge replica

to her scoop of vanilla ice cream. Her eyes flashed to his and he had to work at not laughing.

She looked like a kid who'd been promised cotton candy and instead was handed a lollypop.

"Mmm," he said cheerfully. "Looks good."

"Uh—uh, yes, it looks delicious."

How he loved her! What other woman would smile as if she was really thrilled to pass up a chocolate sculpture for what appeared to be a scoop of plain vanilla?

Karim picked up his dessert fork and sliced into his dessert.

"Fantastic," he said. And then, politely, "How's yours?"

Rachel cleared her throat.

"I'm sure it's wonderful," she said, picking up her dessert spoon, dipping it into the ice cream… "Oh." She smiled with surprise. "There's a chocolate shell under the—under the—"

"Something wrong?"

"No. Well, maybe. There's something inside the shell. It's—it's—"

She went very still.

Karim put down his fork. His heart was racing.

"Cake?" he said, trying to sound calm. "Strawberries?"

She shook her head. "It's—it's…" She looked up again.

Why couldn't he read the expression on her face?

"It's a box," she whispered. "A little blue box."

Suddenly his carefully crafted, oh-so-romantic plan seemed full of holes. Hell, what did he know about what a woman would or wouldn't find romantic?

"Rachel," he said. "Rachel, sweetheart, look, if you want to leave—"

Rachel swallowed hard.

She put down her spoon. Lifted the little blue box from its chocolate shell. Opened it…

A burst of blue-white light seemed to leap from the box to her eyes.

"Karim," she said. "Oh, Karim!"

It was a diamond ring—but that was like saying that the sun was just another star.

The diamond was huge. It looked as if all the fire that had created the universe had been captured within its blazing heart. It was set in white gold, flanked by sapphires that were the exact shade of the sky on a perfect June morning...

Karim watched Rachel's face. He waited for her to say something.

She didn't.

The silence grew.

He wanted to die.

He'd been so careful, selecting the ring when he'd supposedly made a third trip to his office. He knew his Rachel. She would not want anything ostentatious but he wanted something special.

He loved her, and he wanted the world to know it.

He'd spent most of the morning choosing this ring.

Didn't she like it? Didn't she want it? Had she thought things over, changed her mind about him? About becoming his wife?

Calm down, he told himself. Relax. Give her another minute, then say something casual. Say, *I hope you like it.* Or say, *If it's not what you'd have chosen we'll get something else.* Or tell her, *I thought this was kind of nice, but it you don't—*

"Dammit, Rachel," he said in a hoarse whisper, "say something!"

She held the ring in the palm of her hand, looked from it to him.

"It's—it's the most beautiful thing in the world!"

Thank God. "I love you," he said.

"Karim." Tears filled her eyes. "I don't—I don't de-serve—"

He took the ring from her, slipped it on her finger. Yes. It was right. It was perfect. It was beautiful—but not as beautiful as she.

"I love you," he said again, and he pushed back his chair, held her hand, brought her to her feet and took her mouth in a kiss that said, as clearly as words, what he was feeling.

He'd waited all his life for this one woman.

Fate, destiny, karma had meant them to find each other, and to be together for all eternity.

"Rachel," he whispered, and she gave a soft, sweet cry, wrapped her arms around his neck and kissed him back.

"I love you with all my heart," she said through her tears. "I'll always love you. Remember that. Remember that I'll always, always love you."

"*Enti hayati, habibi.* You are my life."

Somebody in the room whistled, somebody else applauded, and Rachel blushed the brightest pink he'd ever seen her blush.

And dazzled him with her smile.

He dropped a handful of bills on the table, led her out into the night and took her home, to their bed, to the private little world that belonged only to them.

They slept in each other's arms.

He woke her during the night and made love to her again. Woke her at dawn to claim her once more.

The next time he woke the room was golden with sunlight. When he saw her lashes flutter, then lift, he smiled.

"Morning, sleepyhead," he murmured.

Rachel smiled. She put her hand against his cheek, rubbing her palm lightly over that deliciously sexy stubble.

"What time is it?" she said sleepily.

He gave her a soft, lingering kiss.

"Time to get showered and dressed, *habibi*. My plane is waiting."

A feeling of dread washed over her. She sat up, the bed-clothes clutched to her breast.

"Your plane?"

Karim tugged the bedclothes away. Bent his head, kissed her breasts.

"We're going home," he said softly. "To Alcantar."

The plane ride seemed endless—far longer than the one from Vegas to New York.

Roberta had come with them. She and Ethan settled com-fortably in the bedroom in the rear of the cabin.

Rachel was full of questions.

"Why didn't you tell me we were flying to Alcantar today?"

Karim laced his fingers through hers.

"I was going to. Then I thought it would only make you nervous."

True enough. She wasn't just nervous, she was terrified. The realization that she was about to meet Karim's father was daunting.

"But what if he doesn't like me?"

Karim put his arm around her and drew her head to his shoulder.

"Sweetheart, he will." He smiled. "Besides, he's been after me for years to find a proper wife."

"Am I a proper wife for you?" Rachel said in a small voice.

He laughed and dropped a kiss on her temple.

"You are a proper wife for any man, but especially for one who loves you as I do." He paused. "I told him about Ethan."

Rachel looked at him.

"And—and what did he say?"

What, indeed? Karim cleared his throat.

"He was surprised, of course. But my father, for all his—what shall I call it?—for all his imperial attitude, my father is a practical man. He is glad he has a grandson."

"But—but he thinks—I mean, he knows that Rami—that I—"

"Yes."

"And?"

Karim hesitated. This was a time for absolute honesty. That was one of the most remarkable things about his relationship with his beautiful fiancée.

They could always speak the truth to each other.

"And," he said slowly, "he will love you as a daughter—once he gets to know you."

She nodded.

"But not yet."

A muscle flickered in Karim's jaw. His conversation with his father had been a difficult one.

"A woman who would bear a son to a man who has not married her," his father had said coldly, "is a woman of questionable morality."

Karim had fought back a hot rush of anger.

"The world has changed, Father."

"Not our world here in Alcantar."

Wrong, Karim had thought.

The world *had* changed, even in Alcantar, and it would change again when he ascended the throne. But there was no sense in arguing the point.

What mattered was making it clear that he would not tolerate any interference in his decision to marry Rachel, or any show of disrespect to her.

"But *my* world has changed," he'd said. "Rachel changed it. I love her and I am proud to take her as my wife."

His father must have heard the steel in his voice because he'd ended the conversation by saying he would see Karim soon.

Very soon, Karim thought, as the plane touched the runway.

The pilot's disembodied voice floated through the cabin.

"We have arrived, Your Highness."

Karim undid his seat belt and Rachel's; he drew her to her feet. Her face was pale and his heart went out to her. Her world was about to change, too.

Alcantar was a beautiful, proud country, but it was surely different from any place she had been before.

And he, once he stepped from the plane, would be different, too.

Perhaps he should have warned her of that, he thought as they reached the door and the steps that led down from the jet.

Too late.

He heard her whispered "Oh!" when she saw the convoy of white Bentleys flying the falcon flag of Alcantar, the uniformed honor guard standing at attention, the pomp and circumstance that awaited them.

"Karim," she whispered, "I don't know if I—if I—"

He put his arm around her. It was a breach of protocol, but to hell with protocol. Rachel was what mattered.

"You can," he said softly.

She leaned against him as if to draw on his strength for one brief second. Then she stood erect.

He was right.

She could do this.

I can do this, Rachel thought.

She could do anything for Karim. It was only that his titles—sheikh, prince, heir to the throne—had, until now, been nothing but words—and that she could not possibly be the perfect wife he wanted because she was a world-class liar.

Okay.

That was over.

If she could do anything for the man she loved, then she could tell him the truth.

He loved her. He understood her.

He'd understand that lying had been her only option.

The decision gave her the last bit of courage she needed.

She forced a smile as he led her down the steps, kept smiling when he paused and saluted the captain of the honor guard. She kept her hand on his arm and wondered if he could feel her trembling.

"All right, sweetheart?" he said softly once they were in the lead car, Roberta and the baby in the second.

"Yes," she whispered.

And thought what a really fine liar she was.

They drove along a palm-fringed road, through a town that looked modern and prosperous, toward an ivory and gold palace that rose against a cloudless blue sky, then made their way through a golden gate, down another tree-lined road and stopped in an enormous courtyard, with the dome of the palace looming above them.

A man in a white *keffiyeh* opened the door of their car and snapped to attention.

Karim stepped out, offered his hand to Rachel. She put her icy fingers in his.

"Everything will be fine," he told her softly. "You'll see."

Everything *was* fine as they walked up the palace steps, Roberta just behind them with Ethan in her arms.

Everything was still fine as they went through its massive gold doors, down a long marble corridor that led not to the throne room but to the King's private chambers.

That surprised Karim. Was it a good sign that his father chose to receive them here, or was it a bad one?

He stopped wondering once they were ushered into his father's enormous sitting room.

The drapes had been drawn against the afternoon sun; the King sat in an elaborate ivory and ebony chair, dark shadows clustered behind him.

Karim could feel the tension in the air.

He kept his arm around Rachel's waist.

"Father," he said.

The King rose to his feet.

"We are not to be disturbed," he snapped to the servant who'd escorted them.

The servant bowed. The door swung shut.

"Father," Karim said, "this is—"

His father held up his hand, looked from him to Rachel. There was icy fire in his eyes.

"This is a woman who saw the perfect way to lure a fool into her bed."

Karim's eyes narrowed. "Listen to me, old man—"

"No, my son. You will do the listening."

As if it were a signal, a woman with long blond hair and bright blue eyes stepped out from the shadows behind him.

Rachel's hand flew to her throat.

"Suki?"

"Damned right," Suki said sharply. "Did you really think you could get away with this, Rachel?"

Karim looked from one woman to the other.

"Rachel? Is this your sister?"

Rachel swung toward him.

"Karim." Her voice shook. "Karim, please… I tried to tell you. I tried so hard—"

Karim felt as if a dark pit were opening at his feet.

"Tell me what?"

"Really?" Suki said, her hands on her hips. "You tried to tell him? I don't think so. I don't think you had any intention of telling the truth, ever. I mean, you couldn't take Rami away from me. Snagging his brother was the next best thing."

Karim stared at Rachel.

"What is she talking about?"

Rachel shook her head.

He clasped her shoulders and drew her to her toes. "Dammit, what does she mean?"

"What I mean," Suki said, "is that my beloved sister worked her ass off, trying to land a guy with money. First at the casino. Then right under my nose."

"Suki," Rachel whispered, "don't—"

"But she couldn't. See, Rami loved me. And then he and I had a silly quarrel." Suki pulled a tissue from the neckline of her tight pink top and dabbed her eyes. "He left me. And I was frantic. I loved him, you know? And he was the father of my baby—"

"What?"

"I asked her if she'd take care of Ethan while I went looking for Rami, but—"

"Is this true?" Karim's voice was hoarse; his eyes blazed into Rachel's. "Ethan is your sister's child?"

Rachel was numb. "Karim," she whispered. "Karim, please—"

"Of course he's mine," Suki said sharply. "And you stole him."

Even in her despair, Rachel wondered why only she could see the glint of malice in her sister's eyes.

"I didn't steal him. You know that. You abandoned him—"

"You mean I trusted you to take care of him while I tried to find work." Suki looked at Karim. "See, after your brother left me—well, I was broke. I couldn't find a job in Vegas. Man, I was desperate. I asked Rachel to take care of Ethan for a while, just for a while, and I went to Los Angeles and finally got hired—"

"It wasn't like that," Rachel said desperately.

"I sent her money each week but she always wanted more. And then she saw her chance. Rami's brother—you, Prince Karim—turned up, and you was rich—even richer than Rami—"

"No," Rachel said in a thin voice. "Suki, don't do this! I beg you—"

Karim's hands tightened on Rachel's shoulders.

"Tell me she's lying," he said in a low voice. "Tell me none of this is true, that the last weeks were not a lie—"

"Karim," Rachel pleaded. "Ethan is hers. But nothing else was the way she makes it sound…"

Karim's eyes filled with pain. He lifted his hands from her shoulders, turned on his heel and walked out of the room.

Suki smiled in triumph. She brushed past Rachel and reached for the baby.

"Precious boy," she cooed, "come to your mommy."

Ethan gave an unhappy cry and Rachel sank to the floor, weeping.

CHAPTER TWELVE

ROBERTA hurried to Rachel and threw her arms around her.

"Please," she said as she helped her to her feet, "Rachel, don't cry! Those things that woman said—"

"What she said about Ethan is the truth," Rachel sobbed. "She gave birth to him... But I'm the one who loves him."

"But the rest was lies. Anybody who knows you would know that." The girl's tone was bitter. "Prince Karim should have known it, too. How could he have believed those things she said?"

It was the question that was breaking Rachel's heart.

Karim had said he loved her, but he'd accepted all Suki's horrible lies. How could he?

The answer was simple.

He'd accepted Suki's story because the core of it was true.

She, Rachel, had lied to him from the minute he'd entered her life. She'd lied about Ethan, about Rami, and now those lies had cost her everything.

The child she loved as if he were her own.

The man she adored.

She'd lost them both, forever.

Oh, she could blame Suki for it. For abandoning Ethan, for telling a twisted story to Karim and his father. She could blame Karim for turning back into the heartless man he had always been.

But the terrible truth was that she had only herself to blame. Not just for lying. For giving in to emotions she had always known were dangerous.

Love was the greatest lie of all.

Lust was what drew men and women together. If only she'd remembered that instead of trying to dress it up…

And after a lifetime of knowing.

"Miss?"

Rachel looked up. It was the servant who'd escorted them to this room, but he was speaking to Roberta, not to her.

"The child…" The man cast a furtive glance at Rachel. "The child's mother needs your help."

"Let her get it from someone else," Roberta said angrily.

Rachel touched her arm.

"Please," she said, "go with him. Help her."

"Help your sister? Are you crazy? She's a—"

"I know what she is," Rachel said bitterly. "But you won't be doing it for her. It's for—for my baby." Her voice broke. "He must be terrified. He's in a strange place with a person he doesn't—he doesn't—" Tears flooded her eyes. She put her hand out and Roberta clasped it in hers. "Please, Roberta," Rachel whispered. "My little boy needs you."

Roberta began to weep.

"Yes. You're right. Don't worry. I'll stay with him as long as they'll let me."

The women hugged. Then Roberta hurried after the servant, and Rachel was alone.

Even the King was gone.

The huge room filled with silence.

Rachel wiped her hands over her wet eyes, uncertain of what to do next. She had to leave this terrible place, but how?

"Rachel."

That deep, familiar voice. She whirled toward the door

and saw her lover. His face was cold with anger but it didn't matter.

She knew that she had just added one lie to another, telling herself what she'd felt for him was only lust.

She loved him.

And she had lost him.

A yawning emptiness stretched ahead. Years alone, without her baby. Without the man she adored.

He stood looking at her, arms folded, eyes narrowed. Still, hope rose within her breast, as bright as the mythical phoenix would surely have been as it rose from the flames.

"Karim," she said unsteadily, "Karim, please, if you'd just listen—"

"That was my first mistake. I *did* listen—to you, and your lies."

"I shouldn't have lied. I know that. But I never lied about us."

His mouth thinned.

"There is no 'us.' There never was."

"I love you, Karim. You have to—"

He held out his hand.

She stared at the piece of paper in it. "What is that?"

"A check."

"A check?" She looked at him blankly. "For what?"

"For a masterful performance. Go on. Take it."

Rachel raised her hands in front of her, as if she were warding off something evil.

"It's for fifty thousand dollars. Not enough?" He shrugged. "How much, then? One hundred thousand? I warn you, Rachel, there's a limit to my generosity."

"Do you really think I'd take your money?" She gave a sad, disbelieving laugh. "I don't want money. I want—"

"You want what you almost had," he said coldly. "My fortune. My title. A child who is not yours."

Each accusation was like a blow.

"That isn't true!"

"You are not a woman to speak of what is and is not true."

"You never loved me at all," Rachel whispered. "If you had, you'd know I don't want money. You'd know Suki made up that entire story. She gave birth to Ethan, yes, but she didn't leave him with me so she could find a job. She left him because she didn't want him. She took off without a word, and I never heard from her again."

"You're fast on your feet," Karim said tonelessly. "As I said, you give an excellent performance."

"Dammit, will you listen? Suki made it all up! I never tried to seduce Rami. I barely spoke to him. Yes. I lied about Ethan. But if I hadn't you'd have taken him from me. Don't you see that?"

"What I see is that you're incapable of speaking the truth."

Rachel stared at Karim. Before her eyes he'd become all the things she'd called him when they'd met: an egotistical, arrogant despot.

How could she have thought she loved him?

Losing Ethan would hurt forever.

Losing Karim was the best thing that could have happened to her.

"And you," she said, "are incapable of being a man. The only thing you're suited for is being what you are. A cold, heartless sheikh!"

She took a deep breath. Then, head high, she brushed past him.

"Rachel!" She didn't answer. He cursed and went after her, dropped a heavy hand on her shoulder and swung her toward him. "No one walks away from me until I dismiss them."

"No," she said quietly, "I'm sure they don't, Your Highness." Her chin lifted. "How would they dare?"

"Watch what you say to me, woman."

"Why? What more could you do to me than you've already done?"

"You are in my country now. My word is—"

Karim fell silent.

Sweet heaven, what was he doing? Yes, she had lied to him. Made a fool of him. Now she was turning him into the very kind of man she'd accused him of being.

What kind of power did she have that she could reduce him to this? That she could make him lose his self-control not only in bed but out of it?

No.

He wasn't going to think about her in bed. Her seeming innocence at the start, her incredible abandon once she was in his arms.

Looking at her even now, knowing she had lied, that she had used him, he wanted her.

And she wanted him. She had to want him. She had to—

"I want to go back to the States."

"What if that isn't what I want?"

"Don't you get it? I don't give a damn what you—"

Karim pulled her into his arms. She struggled; he caught her hands, imprisoned them against his chest.

"Let go of me!"

"What happened in bed," he growled. "Was all that a lie, too?"

She struggled harder. He thrust one hand into her hair, held her to him.

"The sighs. The moans. The things you did, the things you begged me to do—"

"You're disgusting," Rachel said, her voice shaking. "And I hate you. I hate you—"

He kissed her. She fought and he caught her bottom lip

between his teeth, sucked on the sweet flesh, heard her whimper, felt her mouth soften under his—

"Stay in Alcantar," he said. "You can help care for the child during the day, and at night, whenever I'm here—"

She made a wild, terrible sound, pulled back in his arms and spat in his face.

"Stay away from me," she panted. "I swear, if you ever touch me again—"

Karim thrust her from him. The boiling rage within him—at her, at himself—terrified him.

"My pilot will fly you to New York first thing in the morning."

"Now," Rachel demanded.

"He cannot fly without sleep."

"That's your problem, not mine."

"My problem," Karim said coldly, "is making sure I don't have to set eyes on you again." He snapped his fingers; a servant came scurrying into the room, eyes averted. "Show Ms. Donnelly to her suite."

"I am not spending the night under the same roof as you!"

"If you prefer the desert sand to a bed, I can see to it that you are accommodated. I'm sure the snakes and the scorpions will appreciate the company."

He said something in his own tongue to the servant, then strode away, his very walk as supercilious as his attitude.

"Bastard," she hissed.

The look of shock on the servant's face made her feel better.

The thought of spending the night outdoors didn't.

"Where are the Sheikh's quarters?"

"In the north wing, madam."

"Fine," she said briskly. "In that case, please show me to a suite in the south wing."

The servant inclined his head and set off at a brisk pace, with Rachel following after him.

She was sure she wouldn't sleep.

She was too angry.

She'd made a fool of herself, thinking she loved the Sheikh—and thinking it was all she'd done.

Suki had always teased her.

"You're just not normal, Rachel," she'd say. "Not liking guys... What, are you frigid?"

Maybe she was. Or maybe she had been. Karim had changed that. She supposed she should be grateful to him for introducing her to the pleasures of lust, because what she'd felt for him was that.

Pure, basic lust.

Of course, being a strait-laced idiot, she'd had to give a purely primitive sexual need the trapping of romance.

"Stupid," she told herself, as she showered in a bathroom the size of a ballroom, then crept between the covers of a bed that could have slept a basketball team.

Stupid, indeed—and how could she ever expect to sleep, knowing that about herself?

And why was she remembering sleeping in his arms, his breath warm on the nape of her neck, his hand cupped over her breast...

The tears came as a surprise.

What was there to cry about?

Not him. Never him, she thought...

And buried her face in the pillow, to muffle her sobs.

Karim lay sleepless in his bed, arms folded under his head, staring at the dark ceiling.

He was still too angry to sleep.

Tomorrow loomed as a day filled with unpleasantries.

He had to talk with Suki Donnelly. The thought was dis-
tasteful. He'd disliked the woman on sight but he'd have to
see if she was going to grant him custody of Ethan without a
fight. She was the baby's mother, after all. Rachel, who was
only his aunt, had flat-out refused.

He could not imagine the baby's mother would do any
less.

If she did, he would sue for custody. And win. But it would
be simpler if she agreed that letting him become Ethan's
guardian would be the best thing for the child.

He'd also have to arrange for a nanny, since Roberta's
foolish loyalty was surely to Rachel.

And he'd have to confront his father.

He knew exactly what the older man had done. The King
had boasted of it.

"You gave me Rachel Donnelly's name. I arranged to have
her investigated. It took very little time to find out that there
was no record of her having given birth to a child—that there
was, instead, a birth certificate issued to a *Suki* Donnelly.
Locating her was even easier. She had no reason to hide. My
people found her in Los Angeles in less than a day." His father's expression had hardened. "If you'd thought with your
brain instead of your—"

"Watch what you say to me," Karim had growled.

But it was good that these things had been done. Otherwise
he'd still be with Rachel, planning a life with her…

Karim pushed back the blankets, rose from his bed, pulled
on a pair of jeans and paced from room to room in his suite.

It was a very large suite. Still, he felt trapped. Caged, like
a captured wild beast.

How could he have made such a mess of things?

He never did anything before thinking it through to its
logical conclusion. That was the code he demanded of him-

self. He never gave in to selfish wishes, or spoke without weighing every word.

Then he'd met Rachel.

He had wanted her, and he had taken her.

Not so terrible, really.

Sex was sex. You wanted a woman, she wanted you—there was no reason to hesitate.

It was what had come next that had been wrong.

When he'd felt himself falling in love with her he should not have let it happen.

Because it was true. He had fallen in love with her and it had been a terrible mistake.

He should have thought of the consequences, considered where undisciplined emotion might take him, remembered that he was a prince, not a man...

"Oh, God," he whispered as he sank into a chair and buried his face in his hands.

Bad enough he'd fallen in love with her, but he *still* loved her. He would never admit it to anyone but it was true.

He loved her.

He'd get over it, of course, but when? How long would it take before he stopped feeling empty without her beside him? How long would the pain of her deceit last?

This was impossible.

How could he think clearly? He had to get some sleep. Or do something useful.

Ethan.

How was the baby doing? The nanny was with him, but nothing else in the child's world was familiar. New surroundings, new faces.

No Rachel.

So what? His mother—his real mother—had him now. Surely there was something intrinsic in the bond between an infant and its mother...

Karim sprang from the chair, grabbed a shirt and left his rooms.

The palace corridors were long. It was a brisk few minutes' walk to the nursery where he and Rami and generations of royal children had been raised. When he reached it, he paused.

Then he knocked on the door.

Rachel's sister opened the door as quickly as if she'd been expecting him.

"Prince Karim," she purred. "How nice of you to pay me a visit."

She was wearing something long and pink and voluminous. Something that was also sheer enough so he could see glimpses of her body as she stepped back.

He thought of the first time he'd seen Rachel. She'd been wearing that foolish costume, her hair messy, her shoes kicked off. There'd been nothing sexy about her, but her beauty had stolen his breath.

And that first glimpse he'd had of her naked…how he'd deliberately parted the bath sheet she'd been wrapped in, her body lush and damp, her face scrubbed clean…

"Come in, Your Highness," Suki said. She smiled. "I've been hoping you'd come by."

Karim stayed in the doorway and cleared his throat.

"How is Ethan?"

"Huh?"

"Your son. How is he?"

"Oh. Oh, he's okay. Don't you want to come in and stay for a while?"

"I've told the kitchen staff to be sure his usual formula is available, as well as a supply of strained fruits and vegetables, but if you need anything else for him—"

"That girl—Rebecca, Roberta, whatever her name is—she's taking care of all that." Another smile, this time accompanied by a flutter of lashes. "This is really something. The palace, these rooms…" She fluttered her lashes again. "You."

"It must have been difficult for you, being away from Ethan for such a long time."

"Oh, sure. And there's a stocked bar here. I didn't know you people drank wine. I opened a bottle—there's some left. How about I pour us a drink? I don't know about you, but I could sure do with something relaxing after today."

"I don't want anything to drink."

"Uh…okay. You could still come in for a while and—"

"You said you sent Rachel money?"

"Right."

"Did you never phone her? To see how Ethan was?"

"Yes," she said quickly. Too quickly. "Sure I did."

"When?" He could hear the sudden hardness in his voice. "She and I were together for three weeks. Rachel has a cell phone but you never called her once during that time."

"Well, she wanted it that way."

"Rachel did?"

"Yeah. I, uh, I don't want to make her look bad—"

"She didn't want to hear from you?"

"See, she told me how she was doing me this big favor—telling me she didn't have time for taking care of the kid, all it was gonna involve, you know—and finally she said, 'Look, I know you'll be busy job-hunting, so if you send money I'll take care of the kid. Just don't drive me nuts checking up on me all the time.' You know?"

"The kid?" Karim said tonelessly.

"Right. Ethan."

Suki smiled. Licked her lips. The action was deliberate and diversionary; he knew he was supposed to notice it and he did—and thought how repellent her wet mouth looked, and how delicious Rachel's mouth looked when it was wet with his kisses.

"You positive you don't want to come in, Your Majesty?"

Karim didn't consider correcting her. "Majesty" wasn't an applicable title, but what difference would that make in what came next?

It was late, and he knew what he had to do if he was going to get any sleep at all.

He smiled. "On second thought..."

And he stepped inside the room, reached behind him, and closed the door.

CHAPTER THIRTEEN

EVENTUALLY weariness won out and Rachel fell into a troubled sleep.

She woke abruptly, alone in a strange room, with a ceiling fan turning high overhead, rain pounding against the arched windows.

Rain in the desert.

It seemed appropriate.

She sat up and pushed her hair from her face. She'd slept in a T-shirt and panties—not naked as she'd slept in Karim's arms…

She wasn't going to think about him. She'd cried over him last night but he was nothing to her now, just as she was nothing to him.

Her suitcase was on a low ebony bench. She opened it, her movements brisk, her head telling her that if she slowed down that brave thought of a moment ago would give way to despair.

Quickly, she dug out a bra and panties, a change of clothes. Five minutes in the bathroom—a fast shower, teeth brushed, wet hair drawn back in a low, no-nonsense ponytail—and she was dressed and ready.

The only thing she had to do, absolutely would do, was to see Ethan—no matter the objections she was sure Suki and Karim would make.

After that Karim's pilot would fly her home—and where, exactly, was that?

Home, people said, was where the heart was. Ethan was the reason Las Vegas had been home. Karim was what had made New York her safe haven.

Now what?

Rachel sank down on the edge of the bed.

This was foolish.

She was accustomed to being alone. She had been alone before Ethan, before Karim. So what if she was alone again?

She'd be fine.

Needing others was always a mistake. Surely life had taught her that.

If she'd just kept her emotional distance from the baby, if she hadn't let a man steal her heart...

No.

He hadn't stolen her heart. She'd served it up to him on a platter.

"Stop it," she whispered.

It was a waste of time to keep going over and over all this. The idea was to move on. She had to make plans, decide what town, what city she'd go to, then find a place to live, a job—

Someone knocked at the door.

It was probably one of the palace servants, come to tell her the plane was ready. Well, the pilot would just have to wait. She was not leaving here until she saw her baby...

The knock at the door came again.

Rachel ran her hands over her eyes and got to her feet. "I'm coming," she called as she hurried to the door, pulled it open...

Karim.

The sight of him, dressed as casually as she was, in a T-shirt and jeans, his jaw bristling with early-morning stubble, sent a wave of longing straight through her.

He still looked like the man she'd fallen in love with, but he wasn't.

She had to remember that.

"Good," she said coolly. "I thought I was going to have to waste time searching for you."

"May I come in?"

"I don't see any reason for it. What I have to say will only take a minute." She paused, told herself it was important to sound determined. "I want to see Ethan."

"He's asleep."

"I want to see him, Karim, and I'm not going to take no for an answer."

A wave of despair shot through him.

Despite everything, he knew he would miss Rachel. In his bed, yes. But this—this might be what he would miss the most. Her spirit. Her courage. Her determination.

Her eyes were red, as if she'd been weeping; she'd pulled her T on backwards—he could see the tip of the label peeking out of the neckline—so perhaps she wasn't quite as contained as she sounded.

He hoped so.

A woman who lied to a man, who let him think she was what she was not, should have at least some regrets...

His heart hardened.

And what kind of fool was he, to think he would miss *anything* about her?

As for regrets... Of course she had them. She'd lost a big ticket item when she lost him.

"Did you hear me? I want to see—"

"I heard you. The answer is no."

Rachel put her hands on her hips.

"I'm not leaving until I've seen him!"

Karim laughed. It was not a pleasant sound.

"You'll leave when I say—and that's twenty minutes from now."

"I demand—"

"Demand?" he said, his tone silken. "You're not in the position to 'demand' anything."

"Karim. If you ever—if you ever had any—any feelings for me—"

She cried out as he clasped her by the elbows and lifted her to her toes.

"Don't you speak to me about feelings," he growled. "You don't know the meaning of the word."

"I loved you." The words she'd promised herself she would never speak again tumbled from her lips. "I loved you so much—"

"I'm sick of your lies!"

"It isn't a lie. I loved you. I loved Ethan—"

"Yes," he said, letting go of her. "I believe that."

For a second Rachel's heart soared—but it didn't last.

"I believe that you do love Ethan, which is why I've come to talk to you." He paused. "He is going to need a nanny."

"Roberta will—"

"She won't. She'll stay the week but she's enrolled for summer classes in New York."

"Well, Suki will have to manage alone."

Karim's mouth twisted.

"Your sister and I had a talk last night. She's already gone."

"Suki? But—"

"Being given the choice between raising her son and granting me custody turned out to be no choice at all."

"You mean she's letting you keep Ethan?"

"She agreed to sign away her rights and let me adopt him."

Rachel stared at him. "Why would she agree to that?" Her eyes widened. "You paid her off."

He had. That was why he'd agreed to step into the spider's parlor. Suki had expected sex. What she'd gotten was a check for seven figures, an iron-clad document that bound her to silence about Rami, the baby, and anything pertaining to the matter, and a warning never to come anywhere near Ethan again. But he wasn't going to talk about that.

"Let's just say we reached a mutually beneficial arrangement."

"And—and the rest? Did she tell you that she'd lied about me?"

"We didn't discuss you, only Ethan."

Rachel nodded. She could feel the burn of tears behind her eyes. Why would they have talked about her when Karim had believed Suki's lies without hesitation?

"And?"

"And what?"

"And what are you doing here?"

"I thought you would want to know that I will raise Ethan. I assumed that would be important to you—that you'd be happy to know he will be safe."

Tears rose in Rachel's eyes.

"Thank you. That was—that was kind of you. To tell me, I mean."

Karim hesitated.

"You've done a fine job with him," he said softly.

She nodded. "I tried."

"I—I want you to know that I love him."

And me? she almost said. *Can't you love me?*

But he couldn't. She knew that.

He was a man to whom honor was everything, and by lying to him she had dishonored him.

"I know you do," she said. "And that's good." Her voice thickened. "Because he's going to need you, you know? He's only a baby, but—but this is going to be a hard transition for him."

Karim nodded. "I'll do everything I can to make it easier." He hesitated. "I regret the—the suggestion I made last night."

Rachel lifted her chin. "Is that an apology?"

"No. It's—it's…" He sighed. God, she was tough. "Yes. It is. But the fact remains, Ethan will need a nanny. I can find one, of course, but he cares for you, and you for him." Her eyes snapped and he held up his hand. "No. I'm not suggesting… I'm simply saying that if you wanted to be his nanny— only that, nothing more—" Dammit, this was not going well. "You'd have your own apartment in the palace, a significant salary and—"

"You mean, I would be your servant."

"I suppose that is one way to see it," he said stiffly.

"And," she said, her voice trembling, "how long would this arrangement last?"

"Until he is five, perhaps, or six. Until he no longer needs you."

Until he no longer needs you…

Rachel wanted to slap the Sheikh she'd been fool enough to love. That he could even think she'd accept being a temporary part of her baby's life told her everything she needed to know.

"Only a man with no heart would make such an offer," she said quietly. "And I pity you, Karim, for being such a man."

She brushed past him, half expecting him to come after her and stop her. But he didn't, and after a few minutes she found a servant and demanded to be taken to Ethan's room.

The servant said that was not possible. Rachel assured him it damned well was, and finally Karim strode toward them, barked out a command, and the servant bowed, then led her to the room where the baby was, as Karim had said, fast asleep.

She stood over his crib, wept silently, whispered to him

of how she loved him, how she knew he would grow up to be big and smart and strong, promised him that she would fight to get him back.

And then, before she could collapse with grief, she swung away from the child who held her heart in his tiny hands and ran through the palace, down what were surely a thousand steps, and out the front door into the rain.

A car was waiting.

The driver took her to the palace airport. Somehow she held herself together until she was on the plane and in a seat.

"Please fasten your seat belt," the still-polite flight attendant said. "We'll be taking off immediately."

Rachel nodded. She didn't trust herself to speak.

The jet's engines started up.

"We have direct clearance to New York, Ms. Donnelly," a tinny voice said from a speaker.

The attendant made her way up the aisle and vanished into the cockpit.

The jet began rolling along the taxiway.

I am not going to cry, Rachel thought, as she stared blindly out the window at the rain, *I am not...*

Sobs burst from her throat.

She leaned her forehead against the glass, let her tears spill down it.

The sky was weeping and so was she.

The plane moved faster and faster. Another few yards and it would reach the runway; the engines would race as it built up speed.

Then it would leap into the sky and all of this would be over.

Suddenly the pitch of the engines changed from a thunderous roar to a whine.

The plane began to slow.

A car, red and low and moving very, very fast, was racing along the rain-soaked taxiway toward them.

The jet rolled to a stop, engines idling. The co-pilot hurried into the cabin from the cockpit.

"What's happening?" Rachel said. Her voice rose. "I said, what's—?"

But she could see what was happening for herself. The co-pilot began opening the cabin door.

And as he did, the door of the red sports car flew open.

Karim jumped out.

Karim? Here? Rachel was baffled. Why?

The plane's door swung open. The staircase dropped into place.

Rachel fumbled with her seat belt.

She wasn't going to face Karim sitting down. She'd do it toe to toe, and if she had to fight him to leave this awful place—

Karim raced up the stairs, his face tight with anger.

"Damn you, Rachel," he said, and before she could say or do anything he hauled her into his arms and kissed her.

She twisted her head away. She didn't want his kisses, the feel of his arms, the strong, wonderful feel of his body against hers...

And then she sobbed his name, clasped his face and gave herself to him.

"I hate you," she whispered. "Do you understand me, Karim? I hate you, I hate you, I—"

"Don't leave me. I beg you, *habibi,* don't ever leave me."

"I can't stay. Not like this. I'm not going to be your mistress, and that's what I'd end up being because I can't keep away from you. I can't, I can't—"

"I love you."

"You want me. There's a difference."

"Damned right, I want you. I want you because I love you.

And you love me. Say the words, sweetheart. Tell me that you love me, too."

Rachel shook her head. He had broken her heart. All she had left was her pride.

"I don't," she said. "I don't love—"

Karim silenced her with another kiss.

"No more lies," he said fiercely. "Not between us." He clasped her face, lifted it to his. "I've been a fool, Rachel. Of *course* you lied about Ethan. I gave you no choice. I had come to take him from you, and you loved him too much to let that happen." He paused. "Rachel. We belong together. You. Me. Our child. Our Ethan."

"Don't," Rachel pleaded, "don't say things you don't mean!"

"I mean every word," Karim said. "Your sister brought Ethan into this world, but you—*you, habibi*—have been his true mother." He smiled. "As I will be his father." He paused and brushed his lips gently over Rachel's. "I love you," he said softly. "Marry me and be my wife."

"But you believed Suki…"

"I was in agony. I had given you my heart…" His voice cracked. "The heart you say I do not have."

"Karim. Please don't. I said it to—to hurt you…"

"I have a heart, *habibi*. But I learned early to guard it well. It is what happens when people see you only as a prince or a sheikh. They lie. They tell you what they think you want to hear. Even those I loved…" Karim cleared his throat. "Each time my mother came back from wherever she'd gone she promised she would not leave me again, but she always did. And Rami…we were different from each other, even as boys, but we loved each other. Then he turned into someone I didn't know and I—I let him go."

"We can't hold on to those who don't want us," Rachel said softly. "My mother. My sister—"

"Yes. I understand that now. But we—you and I—we want each other. We have each other." Karim smiled. "And we have Ethan. We can be a family, *habibi,* and we can be happy."

Rachel felt her heart swell with happiness. She stood on her toes and pressed a kiss to Karim's lips.

"I hated myself for lying to you, Karim. But I was so afraid I'd lose Ethan, lose you…"

"You'll never lose either of us, *habibi.* Not me, and not our son."

"Our son," Rachel said, and smiled.

Karim kissed her damp cheeks.

"This has been a long journey for me," he said quietly. "When it began, I thought I was learning about Rami. Now I know I was also learning about myself, and about what is important in this world."

"And what is?" Rachel asked softly, though by now she knew the answer.

"Love," Karim said. "Only love matters." He looked deep into her eyes. "Rachel. Will you marry me and be my love, forever?"

Rachel laughed.

"Yes," she said, "yes, yes, yes—"

Karim gathered her in his arms and kissed her, and as he did the rain stopped and the cabin of the plane filled with the brilliant golden light of the sun.

* * * * *

MODERN™

INTERNATIONAL AFFAIRS, SEDUCTION & PASSION GUARANTEED

A sneaky peek at next month...

My wish list for next month's titles...

In stores from 16th March 2012:

- ☐ A Deal at the Altar – Lynne Graham
- ☐ Gianni's Pride – Kim Lawrence
- ☐ The Legend of de Marco – Abby Green
- ☐ Deserving of His Diamonds? – Melanie Milburne

In stores from 6th April 2012:

- ☐ Return of the Moralis Wife – Jacqueline Baird
- ☐ Undone by His Touch – Annie West
- ☐ Stepping out of the Shadows – Robyn Donald
- ☐ Girl Behind the Scandalous Reputation – Michelle Conder
- ☐ Redemption of a Hollywood Starlet – Kimberly Lang

Available at WHSmith, Tesco, Asda, Eason, Amazon and Apple

Just can't wait?

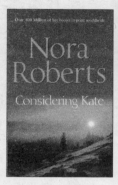

Have Your Say

You've just finished your book. So what did you think?

We'd love to hear your thoughts on our 'Have your say' online panel
www.millsandboon.co.uk/haveyoursay

- 🌹 Easy to use
- 🌹 Short questionnaire
- 🌹 Chance to win Mills & Boon® goodies